Falkirk
**Community
Trust**

**o'ness**
1506 778520

**onnybridge**
1324 503295

**enny**
1324 504242

**alkirk**
1324 503605

**rangemouth**
1324 504690

**arbert**
1324 503590

**Meadowbank**
1324 503870

**Mamannan**
1324 851373

his book is due
r return on or
efore the last date
dicated on the
bel. Renewals
ay be obtained
n application.

Falkirk Community Trust is a charity registered in Scotland, No: SC042403

**Scarlet Wilson** wrote her first story aged eight and has never stopped. She's worked in the health service for twenty years, having trained as a nurse and a health visitor. Scarlet now works in public health and lives on the West Coast of Scotland with her fiancé and their two sons. Writing medical romances and contemporary romances is a dream come true for her.

# HEALING THE SINGLE DAD'S HEART

SCARLET WILSON

MILLS & BOON

Published in Great Britain 2019
by Mills & Boon, an imprint of HarperCollins*Publishers*
1 London Bridge Street, London, SE1 9GF

© 2019 Scarlet Wilson

ISBN: 978-0-263-08072-8

**MIX**
Paper from
responsible sources
FSC® C007454

This book is produced from independently certified FSC™ paper
to ensure responsible forest management.
For more information visit www.harpercollins.co.uk/green.

Printed and bound in Great Britain
by CPI Group (UK) Ltd, Croydon, CR0 4YY

To Auntie Margaret who, thirty-six books in, is still reading and recommending every one of my books to her friends!

# CHAPTER ONE

ON PAPER, THE journey had seemed so long. But for Joe it had been a blink-and-you've-missed-it kind of day. *Go and show your little boy a part of the world where you can make some new memories.* That was what his mother had said to him as she'd handed him the plane tickets to Vietnam.

She had been right. He'd known she was right. And that she was finally giving him the push he needed.

After that, everything had passed in a blur. Getting all their vaccinations, finishing up at work, packing, handing over his house keys to a letting agency and making sure all his mail was redirected to his mother's house.

By the time he'd sat down on the plane he had been well and truly ready for a rest. But his stomach had had other ideas. It had fluttered in a weird kind of way. It had been so long since he'd felt excitement about something he almost hadn't recognised the sensation.

Regan had loved the journey. Between watching movies, eating snacks, sleeping and asking questions he'd been a great travelling companion. And now, as they came in to land at Hanoi airport Regan stared in wonder at the green landscape. 'It's just like home!' he said with a smile.

Joe couldn't stop the ache in his heart. This whole trip was about moving on. He got that. Inside he was ready—up until now he just hadn't quite managed to take the steps. But every now and then Regan did something—it could be a wave of his hand or a look in his eye—that reminded him of Esther. He'd never push away the ache that came from knowing she couldn't see this—couldn't share this moment and be proud of their son and the bright, brave little boy he was becoming.

Joe leaned over and stared out of the window too. He'd half expected to see a city landscape but it seemed Hanoi landing strips were just as green as Glasgow's. Maybe this place would be more familiar than he expected.

The airport was filled with a melee of people. Joe held tightly to Regan's hand as they navigated through passport control and collected their luggage. A guy dressed in a white shirt and casual trousers was leaning against a pillar, holding a piece of paper with their names hastily scrawled in black on it.

*Dr Joe Lennox and son*

He juggled pulling the cases while still keeping hold of Regan as he gave the guy a nod. Around him a dozen languages were being spoken. He just prayed this guy spoke a little English.

'Dr Joe?' the guy asked.

He nodded again. The guy held out his hand. 'Rudi. I'm your ride to the May Mắn Hospital.' He grabbed hold of the two cases and started walking quickly to the exit. 'From Scotland?' he said over his shoulder.

Joe nodded again and bent to pick up Regan, lengthening his strides to keep up.

'I know all the football teams. Which is your favourite?'

Joe laughed. It didn't matter where he went on the
planet, Scotland was known for its football and most
conversations started off this way.

It didn't take them long to hit hectic traffic. It seemed
the whole world travelled by scooter or motorbike in
Hanoi. Regan was tired and tucked in under Joe's arm,
snuggling against his chest.

For the briefest of seconds Joe had a moment of doubt.
What if Regan didn't like it here? He didn't have his
grandparents for reassurance. This was completely different from anything Regan had experienced before. As
he brushed his hand over his son's soft hair, he had a
flashback to Esther. Regan shared his mother's adven-
turous spirit. No matter what they tried, Regan tended
to jump in with both feet. Like most young boys he was
fearless. And that made Joe's heart swell. He didn't ever
want his son to lose that element.

After half an hour Joe couldn't resist winding down
the window in the car to let the sounds and smells of
the city surround them. The first thing that struck him
was how busy the place was, how packed in everything
looked, from people to shops to transport to homes.

Colour was everywhere. They drove by a row of
shops with red, blue and yellow awnings, while packed
above, almost squashed together, were flats.

One was in pink brick, with a balcony on each level,
next door was white, with plants trailing down towards
the awning beneath, next was the thinnest block of flats
he'd ever seen, its first balcony entirely taken up with

a dining table and chairs. Next came a pale blue block, littered with children's toys, then a flat of unknown colour because green foliage completely covered the roof and the outside walls.

It was like a higgledy-piggledy town constructed from a kid's set of building blocks, and it was utterly charming. The area in front of the shops was packed with street vendors, food carts, a variety of tourist souvenirs and brightly coloured long-sleeved shirts. A tiny part of the chaos of the stalls reminded him of the Barrowlands back home in Glasgow. He smiled as he wondered if the street vendors here used as colourful language as the guys back home.

The driver pointed out places as they drove into the Ba Dinh district—then into the French quarter. The French Colonial architecture was evident all around them, but as they passed through, it was clear they were moving further away from the more tourist-oriented areas and out towards the suburbs. It was denser here, street vendors everywhere, but poverty was evident at every turn. A little prickle ran down his spine. Again, it reminded him of home. His GP surgery served one of the most deprived areas of Glasgow.

Children were running happily through the streets, and even though they were still in the city, strips of green occasionally showed. The taxi turned down a slightly wider street. The houses were different here, not as packed in as before. These looked like private residences, each with a little more ground around them.

The taxi driver pulled up in front of a large, pale yellow two-storey French colonial-style house that was a little shabby around the edges. There was a sign just above the door: 'May Mắn Hospital'. The driver turned and smiled, gesturing at the sign and getting out to open the door for them. Joe lifted Regan into his arms and stepped out, letting the close, warm air surround him. 'Bit of a temperature change from Scotland,' he said quietly to himself, turning his head from side to side to take in his surroundings.

There were several similar-style buildings. What once must have been residences seemed to have been converted. Two appeared to be restaurants, another a hotel. It was clear that once the houses had been very grand, though now they all looked a bit run-down. Paintwork was a little faded, some shutters on the windows slightly crooked, and most of the houses gave a general air of tiredness. The only thing that seemed bright was the sign above the door: May Mắn Hospital.

The driver collected their cases from the boot and followed him up the steps to the hospital entrance. He walked through the wide double doors and stopped.

A wave of familiarity swept over him. The smell, the buzz—something he hadn't felt in six months, maybe even longer. Working as a GP wasn't the same as working in a hospital, and the crazy thing about hospitals the world over was that, in some respects, they were all the same.

It didn't matter about the facilities, the climate or the time. The smell of disinfectant, the quiet hum of voices and brisk footsteps made him take a deep breath and let the edges of his mouth turn upwards.

He had missed this. No matter how much he tried to pretend he hadn't. Joe had wanted to be a doctor since he was a kid, and for the last six months...

He swallowed. He'd been working. But he hadn't

been enjoying it. He hadn't loved the job the way he'd once done.

And even though he knew nothing about this place or these people, this felt right.

There was a noise to his right. 'Can I help you?'

He turned to see a woman at his side. She'd spoken English to him. She could obviously tell he wasn't from around here. 'I'm supposed to meet Nguyen Van Khiem, or Nguyen Van Hoa,' he said, trying to say the names in the right order. 'The two doctors that run this place.'

As he spun around to face her, she caught sight of the bundle in his arms. 'Oh,' she said, taking a step back in surprise. She blinked then took a breath.

For a second the air was still between them. He could see the surprise on her pretty face. He obviously wasn't quite what she'd expected. But as his eyes took in her dark hair and eyes, the barest hint of make-up and straight white teeth, he realised that this wasn't quite what he'd expected either. His mother had told him the hospital was run by an older couple with fifty years of experience between them.

The woman spoke. 'You must be the new doctor. Khiem and Hoa told me you should arrive today.' She tilted her head as she tried to catch a look at Regan, who was snuggled into his father's shoulder. 'This must be... Regan, isn't it?'

Now he was intrigued. Who was this woman who'd obviously paid attention to the new arrival?

She was a little shorter than him, with shiny dark brown hair tied back with a clip at her neck. She was wearing a pink shirt and black trousers that showed off her neat waist.

She held out her hand towards him. 'I'm Lien—one of

the other doctors that works here.' Her smile was broad and reached her dark eyes. He must have been looking at her curiously because she filled in the blanks. 'Dang Van Lien,' she said, giving her name in full. 'But the people around here just call me Dr Lien.'

He gave a nod, trying to familiarise himself with saying the family name first. Her handshake was warm and firm. He liked that. She was still holding his hand while she spoke.

'Khiem and Hoa have been called away. They're sorry they couldn't be here to meet you. Come with me. I guess you'll want to put the little guy down.' She reached over and grabbed the handle of both suitcases before he had a chance to stop her and tugged them along behind her.

'Is everything okay?' he asked as he followed her down the corridor, wondering if everything was going to stop before it even started. He was surprised the doctors who had employed him weren't here. 'Where did they have to go?'

She nodded her head. 'They've had to go to one of the other hospitals. It's a few hundred kilometres away, and some of the staff have taken ill. They'll probably be away for the next few weeks.' For a small woman, she had surprisingly long strides. He didn't even get a chance to really see the facilities before she'd led him out the back of the building and pointed to one of three smaller houses set in the grounds at the back. She shot him a smile. 'We're lucky. Good staff facilities here.'

It seemed that the slightly shabby colonial-style house had been hiding some secrets. The grounds at the back were bigger than he would have expected. He hid a smile, likening it to walking into the Tardis in *Dr Who*. There were green bushes, some trees and the three individual white houses set just far enough away from each other to give some privacy. Each of the houses had a different coloured front door, one yellow, one blue and one lilac.

She led him over to the house with the blue door, swinging it open and flicking a switch. She picked up the key that was hanging on a hook behind the door. 'Here you go,' she said as she handed it over.

A warm glow filled the small space. It was cosy. No-where near as big as his house back home. There was a small red sofa in the main room and a table with two chairs, then a neat kitchen set in the back. With a smile Lien showed him the two compact bedrooms, both beds covered with mosquito nets, and bathroom.

It didn't matter that the space was small. There was something about the furnishings and decor that made it welcoming. He laid Regan carefully down on the white bedspread, ensured the mosquito net was in place, then paused for a second and pulled something from Regan's small backpack. He didn't want Regan to wake up with nothing familiar around him.

The picture frame held two pictures of Esther. In one, shortly after delivery, she was pale, holding Regan wrapped in a white blanket, and in the other Esther was much brighter—it was taken a year before her diagnosis with acute myeloid leukaemia and Regan said it was his favourite picture of his mum. In it she was laughing on a beach as her blonde hair blew in her eyes. Joe's fingers hovered over the photo as he placed it on the bed next to Regan's head and backed out of the room, leaving the door open.

'I need a story,' Regan whispered with his eyes still closed.

Joe looked at the stuffed-full cases and Lien caught

his gaze. She gave a little shrug. 'I have a never-ending stack of stories. Why don't you let me tell him one while you try to get yourself settled?'

Something inside him twinged. Telling Regan a bedtime story had been part of their bedtime routine for the last four years. He was tired himself, though, his brain not really computing what time of day it was. Fatigue told him that it might be nice for Regan to hear a story that wasn't one of those he'd repeated time and time again over the years. New stories were in short supply. 'That's really kind of you,' he said. 'Thank you.'

'No problem,' said Lien as she sat at the edge of Regan's bed and launched into a story about dragons.

Joe was actually sad that Regan was so sleepy. He would relish a story like this. Still, it gave him time to open their cases and find their toiletries and some clothes for the next day, along with their mosquito repellent. Everything else could wait.

Lien appeared next to him just as he was trying to shake the creases out of a shirt. 'He's gone,' she said quietly. 'I think he was halfway there when I started.'

Lien moved over to the kitchen. 'Tea?' she asked, holding up a pair of cups. She opened the fridge and a few cupboards. 'Don't worry, Hoa has filled the fridge and cupboards with some staples for you.'

'She has? That was kind of her.'

Lien gestured to the red sofa. 'Sit down. You must be tired.' She gave him a curious look. 'Scotland? Isn't it? You've come along way.'

Joe relaxed down onto the sofa. It was just as comfortable as it looked. He watched as Lien moved easily around the kitchen, boiling water and preparing the tea. The smell drifting towards him was distinctly floral. This wasn't the strong black tea he was used to in Scotland.

A few minutes later Lien handed him the steaming cup of pale yellow liquid. He tried to give an unobtrusive sniff. 'What kind of tea is this?'

She settled next to him, her leg brushing against his jeans. 'The best kind, jasmine. Haven't you tried it before?'

It smelled like perfume, but he wasn't going to say that out loud, so he balanced the cup on his lap and turned a little to face her. 'Thanks for this. You didn't need to.'

'I did.' She grinned, eyes glinting as she sipped her own tea. 'It's bribery. I'm just trying to make sure you'll be fit to work tomorrow. The jasmine tea should relax you a little, and hopefully you'll get some sleep and your body clock will adjust.'

He nodded. 'Ah, bribery. Now I understand.'

She gestured with her hand to the window in front of them. It looked back over to the main building. 'Tomorrow will be busy, a baptism of fire.' She pulled a face and gave a shrug. 'There's some kind of norovirus bug out there right now. We're getting lots of dehydrated kids and adults.'

Joe shuddered. 'Norovirus. Perfect.'

He waited a second then gave her another curious look. 'How long have you been here?'

'All my life,' she replied simply. 'Born and brought up in Hanoi. Trained here, then spent a year in Washington and another in Dublin.' She gave him a smile. 'I wanted to see the world.'

'But you came back?'

She hesitated for a second. 'Of course. I trained with

Duc. He's Khiem and Hoa's son. This local hospital has been here since I was kid. They opened it with some money they inherited, and have kept it running ever since.'

'The government doesn't pay?'

She pulled a face. 'They make a contribution. Hanoi has a population of over six million...' she let out a laugh '...with nearly as many motorbikes. The government is trying to get a handle on our health system, but it's nowhere near as robust as the system in the UK. In most circumstances, you still have to pay to see a doctor in Vietnam.'

'And can the people around here pay?'

She shook her head and held out both hands. 'That's why we're here. We offer free healthcare to anyone who attends. Immunisations for kids. Prenatal health care for mothers. And anything else too.'

Now he'd sat down he realised his bones were actually aching, along with every muscle in his shoulders. Travelling did that to you. The aroma from the tea was strong, vibrant. He took a sip of the hot liquid and tried to let his taste buds acclimatise. He was conscious of the fact that Lien's dark eyes were watching him carefully.

He held up the cup. 'Not too bad.'

She shot him a suspicious glance. 'Well, get used to it. Jasmine tea and iced coffee are the norm around here.'

He lifted one hand to give his tired eyes a rub. 'Your English is great. I'm a bit worried about tomorrow. Let's just say I'm not entirely fluent in Vietnamese. I've learned a few words, but I couldn't hold a proper conversation.'

She shook her head and waved a hand. 'Don't worry. We have a full-time interpreter in the hospital. She'll normally be around to help you. A number of our nurses are bilingual too. You should manage fine.'

She nodded towards the bedroom. 'Have you made arrangements for your son?'

He glanced to the little sleeping figure on the bed. 'Yes, I've registered him at the international school just a few streets over. Khiem had sent me details about it. I've to take him there tomorrow—just before eight.'

'Perfect, it has a good reputation. I'm sure he'll like it.'

She paused once more. 'Khiem said you're here for six months.'

It was a statement, but she said the words like a question. He tried not to let his doubt show on his face. 'That's how long I've taken time off work back home. We needed...' he hesitated, trying to find the right words '...a change of scene. Regan is due to start school back home in six months, so I plan on taking him back for that.' He looked around, realising he hadn't set eyes on any other staff members. 'Does Khiem and Hoa's son work here too?'

Lien laughed. 'Not if he can help it. No, Duc has been lured to the dark side.' She said the words with good humour.

'What do you mean?'

She gave a small shrug. 'He's still doing his round-the-world tour. Getting experience wherever he can. He's a surgeon. This place wouldn't be for him.'

Now Joe was curious at the first part of her answer. 'You said you did the same.'

She put her hand to her chest. 'I just went to two places. That was enough. Got the experience I needed then brought it back here.'

There was something about the way she said those words. He got the impression she was either slightly exasperated by her friend's continued travels, or that she didn't quite approve, but was far too polite to say those words out loud.

'You always wanted to work back here?'

She met his gaze, her brown eyes sincere. 'This is home. I trained to be a doctor to take care of the people that I love.' She held out her hands and gave a soft smile. 'And the people I love are here.'

Something twisted inside his chest. She was talking about herself. He knew that. He understood it. Though he couldn't help but feel the imaginary punch to the guts. He hadn't been able to help the one he loved. There wasn't anything he could have done to save Esther. He'd picked apart every element of her diagnosis and treatment a million times in the long sleepless nights after her death.

As his stomach twisted, Lien gave him a look. She glanced between him and the sleeping form of Regan. 'Why Vietnam?'

Two words. But he knew she was asking so much more.

He swallowed, wishing the tea wasn't quite so scalding so he could gulp it down.

He took a deep breath. He hated it that he'd got used to telling people that Esther had died, seeing their pitying glances or slight discomfort.

'My mother chose it for us,' he said with a rueful smile.

Her brow wrinkled. 'What?'

He lifted one hand and ran it through his hair. A wave of tiredness had just hit him, and he really hoped that bathroom had a shower that he could hit soon. He relaxed back against the sofa. He was too tired for anything but honesty. He didn't have the energy to dress things up.

'My wife died three years ago. It had always been our intention to travel, to show Regan the world, and my mother...' he gave a slow nod of his head '...decided we both needed a change of scene.' He held up one hand. 'Vietnam was one of the places on the wish list.'

'Your wish list, or your wife's?' She hadn't rushed in with an immediate offer of condolence, instead she'd asked an unexpected question.

He shifted a little on the sofa and gave her an interested look. 'It was mine actually. I always wanted to come and work here at some point, it just kind of...fell off my radar.' He paused for a second. 'A lot of things did,' he added quietly.

Lien fixed her eyes back towards the bedroom. 'That's understandable. You had to change your priorities. Becoming mum and dad to a little boy can't have been easy.'

He turned to face her again. He liked this woman. She was direct. They'd only just met but she seemed to read him well. For the last few years people had tiptoed around him instead of having actual conversations with him, just giving him sympathetic glances or a squeeze of an arm.

He closed his eyes for a second and breathed in the warm air of Vietnam. He'd had doubts the whole way here, but now, for the first time, this actually felt like the right move. He smiled.

'Regan makes it easy,' he said. 'I'm lucky.' He shot her a sideways glance. 'I know what happened wasn't lucky, but I still have a part of her. I can see her every day in our son. From a gesture, a look, even his laugh. And I know she would be proud of the little guy.' He let out a deep breath. 'I just hope that this was the right move, at the right time, and Regan will love it here.'

Lien gave an understanding nod as she took a final sip of her tea. 'There's lots to love here, it's a great hospital, and great staff. If you need a hand from any of your colleagues, all you have to do is ask.'

He gave a nod of thanks. The words were reassuring. This was the first time he and Regan had been away from their extended family, and the added complication of Khiem and Hoa not being here when they'd arrived had given him a moment of concern.

He looked back at Lien. 'At the entrance...' he gave a little smile '...you were expecting someone...different?'

Her smile was gentle in return. She knew she'd been caught out. She gave a nod. 'From the description Khiem gave me I was expecting someone...older.' He could see the compassion and warmth in her eyes. 'But you'll do, Dr Joe. You'll do.' She patted him on the shoulder as she stood up and pointed to the fridge.

There was something about the way she said those words that sent a little buzz through his body. The nod of approval meant everything to him and he couldn't quite work out why. Maybe it was the journey, the distance, the unknown. Whatever it was, he could already tell that Lien was someone he could work with. She'd asked a lot of questions tonight and he hadn't really had the opportunity to ask much in return. He was intrigued. He already wanted to know more about his colleague but Lien was talking again.

'There are noodles, vegetables and pork in there. The wok is in the cupboard to the side of the cooker. If you're hungry, you should be able to rustle something up.' She lifted her cup and walked over with it to the sink. 'I can show you where the market is tomorrow if you need to get some other things. It's not too far.'

He stood up quickly, remembering his manners.

'If you need anything, I'm just in the house next door.'

'You are? Which one is yours?'

'Khiem and Hoa stay in the one with the yellow door, and I'm in the lilac one.'

He gave a nod as she opened the door, then realised something. 'Darn it, I haven't even looked around the hospital properly yet.'

Lien waved her hand as she strolled away. 'Plenty of time for that tomorrow. I'll see you in the morning.' She gave him a bright smile as she headed towards the house with the lilac door, her hair bouncing as she walked.

He gave a little shake of his head. He'd been worried. Maybe even a tiny bit scared. But Lien seemed like she could be a good colleague. He looked around the house. It was compact but had everything they needed. Six months.

Six months of something completely and utterly different. And for the second time since his mother had handed him the tickets, he felt a wave of emotion that this time he could recognise. Excitement.

Lien closed the door behind her. Maybe she'd been too direct—too forward. Truth was, she was a little on edge. Khiem and Hoa had expected to be here, but the phone call from the other hospital had meant they'd had to leave at short notice. Joe didn't realise it yet, but it actually meant that they'd be two doctors down for the next few weeks. Lien hadn't been joking about the bribery.

She pulled the clip from her hair and gave her head a shake. She couldn't pretend she wasn't a bit intrigued by the new Scottish doctor. She'd had to concentrate hard at some points when he'd been speaking. Did he realise just how quickly he sometimes spoke, and how the words just seemed to all run into one?

She'd noticed his fingers hovering near the picture he'd placed next to Regan. It was clear it was pictures of his wife. Was he really ready to be here?

She sighed. They'd had doctors here for six months at a time before. The last doctor from Germany had been suffering from mental health problems that had come to a head while he'd been here. A female doctor had come to Vietnam without declaring her drug addiction—something that had quickly become evident. Another colleague had appeared from the US, romanced his way around the staff in the hospital, then left abruptly after three months. Turned out he'd left a wife back home he'd forgotten to tell anyone about.

All three of those doctors had been escaping something, running away from something. It sounded very much like Joe Lennox was doing something similar. Would he really last six months? Because she needed him to. The hospital needed some stability. Sad as his story was, the last thing they needed was another doctor with problems of his own who would leave because he discovered the experience in Vietnam wasn't what he wanted.

She started stripping off her clothes as she headed to the shower. She'd have to help him out as much as she could—particularly until his little boy was settled in the international school. If Joe got cold feet he might decide to get on the first plane home to Scotland. She believed him when he said he'd needed a change. But the fact he'd been honest enough to say his mother had pushed him in this direction bothered her. Was he really ready for this? She hadn't seen his CV. She had no idea what his previous experience was. Khiem and Hoa did all the recruitment and she trusted their judgement. If they thought he'd fit in, then she had to believe that.

But the truth was, it wasn't his skills she was worried about. It was more his heart and his head. If his head was somewhere else he could make mistakes, and if his heart wasn't in it, he wouldn't want to stay.

Something twisted in her chest.

This place meant everything to her.

For lots of the residents in Hanoi, this was their only accessible healthcare. Yes, services were pushed. Yes, they didn't always have all the supplies that they needed. But she was determined that this place would always serve the population that needed it.

People like her, and her family.

This was her city, her people.

And no matter how much empathy she had for the new doctor's circumstances, he had better be prepared to pull his weight around here.

# CHAPTER TWO

LIEN WAS WAITING for him when he arrived back after dropping Regan at the school. He'd obviously been nervous about leaving his son at the strange school in an unfamiliar city, but the place had given him good vibes. The nursery teacher had shown them into a bright, welcoming environment filled with a host of happy-looking children chattering in different languages.

Regan had tugged at his hand after a few minutes, anxious to go and join in the fun, so Joe had left with reassurances that they would call the hospital if there were any concerns.

By the time he got back to the hospital it was a few minutes before eight o'clock. Already the place was a hive of activity. The waiting room had only a few seats left. Lien was wearing a pale blue shirt and navy trousers, and her hair was in a ponytail again. There was no sign of the traditional white coat.

He'd swithered for a few moments this morning over what to wear, before settling on a pair of dark trousers and a simple short-sleeved white shirt. The temperature here was much warmer than he was used to, and he wasn't sure if the hospital had air-conditioning or not. He hadn't noticed last night. He gave a sniff. He wasn't quite used to the aroma of the insect repellent he'd covered both himself and Regan in this morning. Maybe he should have tried to drown it out with more aftershave?

Lien gave him a brief nod as he walked back through the main entrance. 'Good. Is Regan settled?'

He gave a brief nod and she started speaking again straight away. 'Come with me, and I'll give you a walk around. I'll show you our systems and our supplies and when Mai Ahn, our translator, gets here, I'll assign her to you for the rest of the day.' She walked him over to a sink and started washing her hands. He quickly followed suit. She'd already mentioned norovirus problems. Hand washing was one of the key practices to help prevent the spread.

Joe barely had time to draw breath. 'First thing,' Lien said as she kept scrubbing her hands, 'you should really wear long sleeves. If your shirts are too warm, I'll show you a place where you can buy some lighter weight clothing. Do you have your insect repellent on?'

He nodded and she kept talking. 'With Khiem and Hoa away, we're two doctors down. I can't afford for our latest recruit to pick up something from a mosquito bite.'

It felt like a bit of a reprimand and he wasn't quite sure how to react, but Lien was already talking again. 'Hoa covered antenatal and maternity care, so we'll all have to pick up her role while she's gone.'

Joe didn't miss the way that she'd phrased that. She hadn't asked him about his experience, or if he was happy to cover this area. She was letting him know what was expected of him. It seemed her directness last night hadn't been unusual but the norm.

As they finished scrubbing their hands she kept talking while she dried hers. 'Okay, I'm sure you've done

some general reading on the health issues in Vietnam.'
She shot him a sideways glance. 'Or at least I hope you
have.'

He nodded quickly. 'Of course. Main issues are malaria, tuberculosis, HIV and AIDS, with some cases of
dengue fever and ongoing issues with Agent Orange.'

She gave an appreciative nod and held out her hands.
'Biggest killer of kids in our area is malnutrition, cou-
pled with diarrhoea and vomiting. They have no extra
fat layers to fall back on. It hits hard and fast.'

'So a norovirus outbreak is your worst nightmare?'

'Pretty much.'

She led him down one corridor and then up a set of
stairs. 'Okay, downstairs is basically our clinic area.
Upstairs we have six four-bed rooms with a variety of
patients. Children and adults.' He could see how the lay-
out of the traditional colonial house had been adapted
to work as a hospital. There were a number of nursing
staff upstairs to whom she introduced him quickly. The
staff seemed friendly, and the patients well-cared-for.
Most were on IVs. Lien caught his gaze.

'We have a mixture of dehydration in both the young
and the elderly. Lots of chest complaints too. Anyone
suffering from diarrhoea is cared for separately in one
of the single rooms at the other end of the corridor.'

Joe nodded. He'd known whole hospital wards closed
because of winter vomiting bugs. They couldn't ignore,
or not treat, people affected, but, because it was infectious, it had a real chance of being passed to other patients or staff. Hygiene issues had to be the top priority.

'Anyone today that you're worried about?'

She gave him a half-smile. 'I've already done a ward
round this morning, but we'll do another one later so

you can familiarise yourself with the patients. Today we start downstairs at the clinic.'

They washed their hands again, and moved back down the stairs.

Downstairs was separated into four areas. One was a general waiting room, one was for children, one for pregnant women and a fourth for X-rays, with a plaster room next door. It was a real mixed bag. A kind of cross between a GP surgery and community hospital back in Scotland.

Lien gave a little sigh as she showed him into an office and gestured for him to sit in the chair opposite her. 'We have a real mixture of antenatal care. Only around sixty per cent of women in Vietnam attend antenatal care. Some women don't present until late in pregnancy. Others present early, requesting their pregnancy be monitored all the way through for birth defects. It's not unheard of for a pregnant woman in Vietnam to have up to twenty scans.'

Joe's eyebrows shot upwards. The norm for the UK was two, unless there were any concerns. Something clicked in his brain. 'Agent Orange?'

She nodded.

'How often nowadays do women present with birth defects?'

Lien's face was serious. 'It's more prevalent now in the south of Vietnam, but forty years on there are still children affected here. The spray that was used to destroy the crops obviously went into the soil. Poverty is a major issue in Vietnam and some families are solely reliant on growing their own foods. They have no other option but to eat the food they grow—whether the soil is damaged or not.'

She shook her head. 'We have two other hospitals. One is in the outskirts of the city of Uông Bí city, in northeast Vietnam, and the other—the one Duc's parents have just gone to—is in Trà Bồng District in the south of the country. At that one, we also take care of the kids in the nearby orphanage. A lot of them are affected. There's poverty across Vietnam, just like there's poverty in every country in the world, but it's worse down in the south. Down there, families are reliant on farming. If their crops fail, it's disaster for them. A lot of them rely on their kids to work alongside them. If their kids are affected by Agent Orange, or any other genetic or medical condition, often the family can't afford to keep them.'

'So they end up in the orphanage?' Joe asked.

'Exactly. We offer free medical care to the orphanage. Things have improved in the last few years, but we still aren't where we should be.'

'Sometimes I forget how lucky we are in the UK. Yes, things aren't perfect. But the healthcare part of the job generally always gets done.' He gave a slow nod. 'And the first hospital you mentioned?'

'The other is in Uông Bí in Quang Ninh province, in northeast Vietnam, more towards the coast. We'll cover both hospitals at some point in the next six months— generally just for a week or two to cover holidays.'

'Okay.' He was beginning to get a general feel for the place, for the sort of patients he'd be seeing, and the kind of responsibilities he'd have here. None of it seemed beyond his ability, though he'd have to do a bit more background reading on some treatments.

Lien ran through the paperwork they used, how to order tests and their prescribing arrangements. She handed him a pre-printed list with Vietnamese names for some of the more commonly used drugs. It was clear she'd familiarised foreign doctors with the clinic workings before.

Joe leaned on one hand. Everything seemed straightforward enough. 'This place,' he said, 'it's like a cross between a community clinic, a cottage hospital and an ER.'

Lien was watching him with careful eyes. He couldn't quite work out what was going on in her mind. He was sure she was part vetting him, part examining his motives. It was only natural. She was looking for someone she could rely on. Having to check another doctor's practices would be almost as bad as not having a colleague at all. 'Let's hope you don't have to cover it all at once,' she said softly.

He could see the flash of worry in her eyes. But the only way to earn the trust of a colleague was to prove himself. Joe was willing to do that. Back home everyone trusted him in his current role, but he wasn't back home any more. He was in an entirely different country, and while some health needs would be the same, there were others he'd need to query, and Joe wasn't too proud to do that. He would never put patients at risk.

'Where do you want me?'

Lien's eyes brightened at the question. Was that relief he'd just spotted? 'What do you prefer?' she asked. 'I need someone to cover the children's clinic, and someone to cover the adult clinic.'

He gave a nod. The clinic work, whether it was for children or adults, would be very much like his GP role back home. He shot her a smile. 'Happy to do either.' Then met her gaze. 'Put me wherever I can be of most use.'

She shifted a little in her chair, caught off guard at his words. He almost let his smile broaden. She liked being straightforward and so did he. 'I'm not here to be a hindrance, Lien, I'm here to be a help.'

She reached up and brushed an errant strand of brown hair behind her ear that had escaped her ponytail. She was close enough that he could see just how smooth her skin was. She wore very little make-up. But she didn't need any, her dark hair and eyes complemented her appearance beautifully. In another life, in another place, he would definitely have looked twice.

It had been so long since a thought like that had even entered his head that he automatically frowned. What was wrong with him? Where had that come from?

Lien tilted her head. 'Something wrong?'

He shook his head too quickly. 'No, nothing.' He pushed himself up from the chair. 'Where do you want me?' He was anxious to get this day started.

The few seconds of silence was slightly uncomfortable. He flashed back to being a junior doctor and the nurse in charge of the ward shooting him a glance to say she doubted he should even actually touch a patient.

A figure appeared in the doorway and Lien stood up. 'Perfect. Mai Ahn, this is Joe. Joe, this is Mai Ahn, your interpreter. She'll help you with the children's clinic.'

'Children's clinic it is,' he said with a nod, before reaching out to shake hands with Mai Ahn. 'Lead the way.'

She was unsure of him. Of course she was. Did he even notice he occasionally glanced at his mobile clipped onto his belt? It was only natural that he was worried about how his son was settling in on his first day of nursery, she only hoped it wouldn't distract him from the job he had to do.

The children's clinic wasn't for the faint-hearted.

She couldn't help but be automatically protective of the place she loved working in. At least he'd been honest last night. He'd told her that he and his son needed a change after losing his wife. He'd said it had been three years. But she'd seen the glint of pain in his eyes. Was he really ready to move on?

She still had doubts.

It was a shame. Because he was undoubtedly handsome. The burr of the Scots accent was almost melodic—even though she had to concentrate hard. And it was clear that he doted on his son. Just as she'd expect him to.

She gave herself a shake. It was a ridiculous observation. She was used to doctors coming here on short-term contracts, and she'd never considered any kind of relationship. She was too busy. Too dedicated to her work. She'd had her heart broken once, and that was enough for her.

*Too poor.* Not the words he'd used, but those were the words he'd meant. Lien had never pretended to be anything she wasn't. As a child she'd always been well mannered and as well presented as she could be. She'd been bright, and her teachers had noticed. They'd encouraged her to study hard, and eventually helped her to seek out scholarships so she could attend medical school.

At medical school she'd got along with most of her classmates. Reuben had come from a rich family in another city. He'd never asked her where she lived—he'd just made assumptions. Then, when he'd found out, after two years, she'd been dumped quicker than a hot brick.

Her family was proud of her, and she was of them. She'd hated the way it had made her feel. Not good enough. Not rich enough.

She came from one of the poorest areas in the city. Her family still lived there—no matter how much she'd tried to assist them since she'd qualified as a doctor. But even now they wouldn't accept any financial help from her.

They liked where they lived. They still worked hard. They didn't want change, in any form.

Lien lifted the pile of patient notes from the desk. They were all people who were due back at the clinic today to be reviewed.

One of the nurses gave her a smile as she walked into the waiting room. There were already ten people waiting. She gave a nod of her head and smiled, speaking in Vietnamese. 'Okay, who is first?'

The only person having trouble concentrating today was her. She kept casting her eyes through to the other waiting room. She knew that Mai Ahn, the interpreter, would come and find her if he had any concerns. But she didn't. Instead, she saw an occasional glance of Joe carrying babies and toddlers through to the examination room for assessment or vaccinations. Through Mai Ahn, he chatted to the mothers. Most of them seemed happy to talk to him and from the looks on their faces the Scottish doctor was proving a hit.

After a few hours he came through and knocked on her door.

'Lien, can we have a chat about a child?'

She nodded, pleased that he'd come to talk to her.

'I think I've got a little one with complications of tuberculosis. I can't find any previous notes, and there's no X-ray.' His brow wrinkled. 'Don't most babies get immunised against tuberculosis shortly after birth?'

'They should. Unfortunately, tuberculosis is common around here. If babies are born in hospital they are immunised if the parents consent. But not all babies are born in hospitals. What do you think are the complications?'

He ran his hands through his hair. 'She's losing weight, even though she's feeding. Her colour is poor, she's tachycardic, and I suspect her oxygen saturation isn't what it should be. Her lungs don't sound as if they are filling properly. She has a temperature and a cough. I suspect a pleural effusion. Do you have a paediatric monitor I could use while I order a chest X-ray?'

Lien stood quickly and gave him a serious kind of smile. 'Let's do this together.'

He raised one eyebrow. 'Don't you trust me?' He didn't seem annoyed by the fact she was effectively second-guessing him. He might even have looked a little amused.

'You asked for a second opinion, Dr Lennox. I'm going to give you one.'

The amused look stayed on his face. 'Absolutely. I haven't seen many kids with tuberculosis in Scotland.'

She gave a nod as they walked through to the paediatric treatment room. As soon as they reached the door, Lien could almost verify his diagnosis. She switched to Vietnamese and introduced herself to the mother and her five-year-old daughter, who was clearly sick.

Joe's notes were thorough. Three other members of

the family had active tuberculosis. Only one complied with their treatment. It was no wonder the little girl was affected.

Five minutes later they were looking at a chest X-ray. Joe was right at her shoulder. She held her breath and caught a slight whiff of the aftershave he was wearing, even though it was overshadowed by his insect repellent. She wanted to know if he'd recognise what she needed him to on the X-ray.

She needn't have worried. He lifted one finger and pointed to the film. 'Pleural effusion without any parenchymal lesion.' He didn't finish there. 'I know there's some mixed feelings, but because of how this little girl has presented, I would be inclined to drain the effusion rather than leaving it.'

She took a few minutes to recheck things. This was the first time he'd seen a child with tuberculosis, never mind the added complications, and he'd picked it up straight away. She couldn't help but be impressed.

She turned to face him. 'I think you're right. Let's put our public health heads on and try to persuade the rest of the family to comply with their medications. We can use a sample of the effusion to diagnose the tuberculosis. A pleural biopsy would likely be too traumatic right now.'

He nodded in agreement. She paused for a moment, wondering whether she should question his skill set any further.

'Any experience of doing a pleural effusion in a five-year-old?'

He nodded. 'I specialised in paediatrics before training as a GP.' He gave her a steady look. 'I've got this. But I'm happy for you to stay if you'd like.'

He didn't seem defensive or annoyed, but it felt like

a bit of a line in the sand. He already knew she'd questioned his diagnosis. Now she'd asked about his experience. Lots of other clinicians that she knew might have been annoyed by this, but Joe just seemed to have accepted her actions without any discomfort. Still, the tone in his voice had changed a little, as if he was getting a bit tired of her.

She pressed her lips together. If he'd expressed any anxiety about the situation she would have been happy to take over. But he hadn't, and she knew it was time to step back. She had enough patients of her own to see still in the waiting room.

She glanced at the nurse and interpreter. She had confidence in both of them. Either of them would come and find her if they were worried. She tried her best to look casual. 'I'll leave it with you. Shout if you need anything.'

Joe watched her retreat, knowing exactly how hard it was for her. Was his counterpart a bit of a control freak? Or maybe she just second-guessed everyone she worked with?

He tried to understand, even though he couldn't help but feel a little insulted by her lack of faith in him. It's not like he hadn't experienced this himself. He'd worked with plenty of other doctors, in a variety of settings over the years, and it always took a bit of time to reassure himself about a colleague's skills and competencies.

It was clear she loved this place. She'd more or less told him that already. There was also the added responsibility of her employers not being here right now, so the well-being of May Mắn hospital was really in her hands.

He gave some instructions to the nurse, who seemed

to understand his English, then knelt down beside the little girl and her mother with Mai Ahn, the interpreter, to explain what would happen next.

Thirty minutes later the procedure was complete, with some hazy yellow fluid in a specimen bottle for the lab. The little girl's cheeks and lips had lost their duskiness, the oxygen saturation monitor showed improvement, and when he listened to her chest he could hear the improved inflation of her lung. He gave instructions to the nurse for another X-ray, and to further monitor for the next few hours.

'I'll come back and have a follow-up chat about the medicines,' he said. Something came into his head. 'Do doctors make home visits here?'

The nurse frowned for a second as if she didn't quite understand what he'd said, then shook her head. 'No. Never.'

Joe sat back in his chair for a moment. He didn't want to send this child home with just a prescription in her hand. The rest of the family were important too. The mother had already told him that both her husband and father-in-law kept forgetting to take their tuberculosis meds. Only her own mother remembered. If he could just see them, and persuade them how important it was, it might stop other family members being infected. He glanced out to the waiting room. He still had a whole host of patients to see, some of whom would need vaccinations, and some might need tuberculosis testing. He went to the waiting room with Mai Ahn to call the next patient, while his idea continued to grow in his head.

'He went where?'

Ping, one of the nurses, shrugged. 'He talked kind

of strange. Something about a home visit. Apparently they do them in Scotland a lot. He persuaded Mai Ahn to go with him.'

Lien walked over and looked at the notes, checking the address on the file, then grabbed her jacket. She'd nearly made it to the front door, when her brain started to become a bit more logical. All she was feeling right now was rage. She went back and scanned the rest of the notes, checking to see what other family members were affected. 'Did he take prescriptions, or did he take the actual medicines?' she asked Ping.

Ping gave her a smile as she carried on with her work and brought a single finger to her lips. 'I couldn't possibly say.'

Lien nearly exploded. It was obvious that the Scottish charm was already working on her staff. What on earth was he thinking? They had to account for every dose they used. They weren't a dispensary. On a few occasions they gave out enough medicines to see a patient through the night, but they didn't give out medicines on a regular basis.

She snatched up her bag and made her way out into the streets. It was around six now, and the pavements were filled with people making their way home from work, the streets filled with traffic. She did her best to dodge her way through the crowds and cross the few streets. The home address wasn't too far away, but the walk did nothing to quell her temper.

By the time she'd reached the address her heart was thudding in her chest. This wasn't exactly the best part of town. She had no idea how he'd managed to persuade Mai Ahn to bring him here, but she would make sure it wouldn't happen again.

The house was on the second floor of an older block of flats, where each storey looked as if it squished the flats beneath it even more. She climbed the small stairwell and walked swiftly along, checking the number before she knocked on the door.

'It's Dr Lien, from the hospital,' she said.

She held her breath for a few moments, and then frowned. Was that laughter she heard inside? The door creaked open and the elderly grandmother of the household gave a little bow as she ushered Lien into the house.

Lien walked through to the main room, where the majority of the family was sitting on bamboo mats on the floor, Joe amongst them.

Mai Ahn was by his side, translating rapidly as he spoke. He had laid the complicated drugs for tuberculosis out in front of the elderly grandfather, instructing Mai Ahn to draw a paper chart with dates and times.

Lien stopped the angry words that were forming in her mouth. Back when she'd worked in the US, dispensary boxes had been commonplace for patients who were on several drugs. But they weren't widely used here at all. That was what he was doing. He was making a do-it-yourself chart and placing the individual tablets on it.

He looked up and caught her eye. 'Lien, oh, you're here.' His eyes shot protectively to Mai Ahn, whose face revealed she thought she was in trouble. The little girl from earlier was sitting curled into her mother's lap. She'd done well, had been sent home with a prescription for her own meds, and if they were administered to her, she should do well.

Joe stood up. 'I was just explaining to the family the

problems with drug resistance and how important it is to keep taking their medicines.'

There was a shout behind Lien and she turned to see another two children playing in another room. She swallowed and took a deep breath. 'This might be common practice for Scotland, Dr Lennox, but it's pretty unconventional for Vietnam.'

He stood up casually and shook hands with the grandfather, and then the little girl's father, who also had a chart in front of him. He nodded towards Mai Ahn to get her to translate for him again. 'Thank you so much for seeing me.' He nodded to the little girl's mother. 'Make sure you collect that prescription tomorrow, and if you think there are any problems, feel free to come back to the clinic and see me again.' He gestured towards the kids in the other room. 'And remember to come in for the testing. Remember, we can vaccinate too.'

Lien didn't know whether to be angry or impressed. He hadn't just covered the delivery of the prescriptions, he'd covered the public health issues they'd talked about earlier, taking into account multi-resistant TB, contact tracing, further testing and immunisations.

She bowed in respect to the family and spoke a few extra words of reassurance before leading the way out of the house. She waited until the door had closed behind them, and Mai Ahn had hurried on ahead, before spinning around to face him. 'What on earth were you thinking?'

His brow creased. 'I was thinking about patients and their medicines. I was thinking about stopping the spread of disease.'

'We don't do this.' She almost stamped her foot. 'We don't visit people at home.'

He held up his hands. 'Why not? Particularly when it's a public health issue? That mother told me back at the clinic that both the father and grandfather were struggling with their meds. You don't need to be a doctor to know that's how the little girl got infected. What about those other two kids? I didn't even know about them before I got here. Are we just supposed to sit at the clinic and wait another few months until they turn up sick too?'

She could see the passion on his face. It was the first time she'd seen him worked up about anything. 'Have you any idea about this area?' she shot back. 'Have you any idea about any of the areas around here—how safe they are?' She wrinkled her nose. 'Aren't there places in Glasgow city that you shouldn't really walk about alone?'

Now he frowned. 'But you walked here alone,' he said.

She threw up her hands. 'But I'm from here,' she emphasised. 'You,' she said, pointing at him, 'are clearly not.'

She was furious and he'd obviously played this wrong.

Joe looked down at his trousers and the long-sleeved shirt he'd changed into. He knew with his tall build, pale skin and light brown hair he must stand out like a sore thumb. But instead of venting more frustration on his new workmate, he took a different tack and gave her a cheeky smile. 'I don't know what you mean.'

He watched her erupt like a volcano. 'It's not funny!'

Maybe he should wind it back in. He leaned against the wall and folded his arms. 'No, you're right, it's not. But neither is the fact that there could be two more children in that household with tuberculosis and two adults risking developing drug-resistant tuberculosis.' He gave

a sigh. 'I'm just trying to do my job, Lien. I know things
are different here. I know the systems aren't the same
as the UK. But I still want to treat patients to the best
of my ability.'

There was a noise in the stairwell beneath them, and
Mai Ahn rushed back up towards them with a stricken
expression on her face. She muttered something to Lien,
whose face became serious.

She turned swiftly. 'Other way,' she said quietly,
pointing to the stairwell at the opposite end of the pas-
sage.

'Something wrong?' he asked, as the women hurried
ahead of him.

Lien's expression was a mixture of worry and anger.
'You've made us a target, Joe. A Western doctor—
rumoured to be carrying drugs in a poor area of town—
is always going to cause problems.'

A cold shiver ran over his body. He hadn't thought
about this at all. He tried to relate this to back home.
Would he have gone out alone to one of the worst areas
in Glasgow? He didn't even want to answer that question in his head, because the truth was that he had done
it before, and would probably do it again. Some parts of
Hanoi didn't seem that different from Glasgow. But he
hadn't meant to put either of his new colleagues at risk.
Anything he could say right now would just seem like
a poor excuse. He followed them both, turning rapidly
down a maze of side streets until they were back on one
of the main roads.

Lien didn't say another word to him until they reached
the hospital again. A reminder sounded on his phone and
he pulled it from his pocket.

'Apologies, Lien, I need to collect Regan.' He hesi-

tated for a second, knowing that things couldn't be ignored. 'Can we talk about this later?'

Lien's face remained stony. She gave a nod to Mai
Ahn. 'Thanks so much, I'll see you tomorrow. Sorry
about the extra work today.'

The words felt pointed. Part of him was cringing and
the other part was annoyed.

Lien turned back to face him. 'I'll walk with you,'
she said firmly.

It was clear he was about to be told off. First day on
the job and he was already in her bad books. It wasn't
the best start. He could easily defend his position, but
did he really want to get onto the wrong side of his work
colleague, who was also his next-door neighbour?

He decided to be direct, since Lien seemed to like
that approach herself. 'I'm sorry about today. I wasn't
aware there are areas in Hanoi that aren't particularly
safe. I shouldn't have taken Mai Ahn with me. I'll get a
better grasp of the language soon.'

He could see her grip tightening on the handle of her
shoulder bag. 'You shouldn't have gone at all, Dr Lennox.' Her voice was clipped.

He took a deep breath, resisting the urge to snap back.
'You should let me know now—since we'll be working
together for the next six months—are you always going
to call me Dr Lennox when you're mad at me, and Joe
all the other times?'

She must have been expecting some kind of argu-
ment, because his response made her stumble for just a
second. She stopped walking and looked him in the eye.
'Why do you do that?'

'Do what?'

People were stepping around them in the busy street.

'Try and interrupt my train of thought.'

He gave a half-smile. 'Because your train of thought was going down an angry rail. Can we pause at a station and back up a bit?'

She shook her head at his analogy.

He shrugged and held up his hands. 'What can I say? I'm the father of a four-year-old. Train and spaceship examples are the ones that usually work.'

She closed her eyes for a second. Her grip on the bag was becoming less pinched. When she opened her eyes again, her pupils were wide. 'You don't get it,' she sighed. 'The staff and patients at the hospital are my responsibility. Mine.' She put her hand on her chest. 'Can you imagine if I had to phone Khiem and Hoa and tell them that our new doctor had been attacked on his first real day of work and now wanted to head back home to Scotland?'

His hands went to his hips. 'Do you really think I'm the kind of guy to leave at the first hurdle?'

Her gaze was steady but sympathetic, and he could tell from that glance alone that she *did* think that about him. Disappointment swelled in his chest. Her voice was hushed on the crowded street. 'What if that first hurdle results in Regan having no parents?'

He flinched as if she'd just thrown something at him. The words were harsh. They were also something that he hadn't even considered.

Ever. He'd spent the first year after Esther had died wrapping his son in cotton wool, worrying about every minor accident, rash or childhood sniffle. In every thought his worst-case scenario had always been about something happening to Regan—not about something happening to *him*.

He stood for a second, not quite sure how to respond, and then he just started walking, lengthening his strides as he hurried to reach the nursery.

All of a sudden he had to set eyes on his son again. He'd already paid a quick visit at lunchtime, spending his break time with his son and making sure he was settled and happy in his new nursery school. But that had been five hours ago.

Lien walked in short, brisk steps alongside him. If she was struggling to keep up she didn't complain.

'I'm sorry,' she muttered. 'That came out a bit…'

'Wrong?' He raised his eyebrows.

'Direct,' she countered.

'Is crime around here really that bad?' he asked. His brain was whirring. He'd read a lot about Vietnam before coming here—although most of what he'd read had been health related. He couldn't remember reading anything about crime.

'No,' she admitted. 'Hanoi isn't any worse than any other major city. But home visits by doctors are just not done here. Particularly when the doctor might be taking out medicines to patients. Surely you can see that if word got about, it could be dangerous for you, and for anyone around you.'

He wasn't happy. 'So you exaggerated?'

She pressed her lips together. 'I protected my staff,' she said.

'Then who was at the bottom of the stairs?'

'Some members of a local gang. Mai Ahn and I know them, they've attended the hospital before—usually for emergency treatment, you know, stitches for fighting or stab wounds.'

The flare of anger abated. Maybe she hadn't been

exaggerating after all. 'Surely they wouldn't hurt you, then?' he asked carefully.

Her gaze met his. 'But they would probably hurt you,' was her reply.

He swallowed. It seemed he'd need to get to know this city a little better. In Glasgow even the worst kind of people would generally leave a doctor alone. Most people had a moral code when it came to healthcare professionals, knowing that they would likely need help from them one day. But there had been attacks. One of his good friends had been assaulted and his bag stolen when he'd been visiting a terminally ill patient, so it did happen.

She sighed and put her hand up, tugging her ponytail band from her hair and shaking it out. 'Sorry, headache,' she explained. 'They probably wouldn't hurt you. But the truth is I do know them, and they drink. Heavily. They're all fairly young, and some of them think they have something to prove.'

'So you were erring on the side of caution?'

She gave him the first smile he'd seen since she'd come looking for him. 'That's the polite way to say it.' She shook her head again as they approached the international school. 'I'm not trying to scare you off. This is a fantastic city. But like all cities, there is good and bad, and until you familiarise yourself a little better, or at least get a hang of the language, can you try not to get into trouble? Believe me, I've got enough to worry about without having to check on you.'

She was trying to pretend the words were light-hearted but he could sense the sincerity behind them. They reached the door of the school. 'Can you give me five minutes?' he asked.

She nodded and waited outside as he went in to col-

lect an excited but tired Regan, getting a full report
from his teacher.

He walked back out with Regan in his arms. 'It seems
nursery was a big success,' he said with a smile, conscious of how relieved he felt. Knowing that Regan had
had a good day always made him happy. He'd be able
to text his mum and dad tonight to tell them that things
were good, and he knew they'd be relieved too.

'Tell you what, let me try and make amends. How
about I buy you dinner?'

Lien looked a bit surprised. 'Dinner?' she repeated.

He nodded and looked around. 'You choose. Somehow I haven't managed to get to the market today, and
we devoured the food in the fridge last night. Show us
somewhere we can eat on a regular basis.' He raised one
eyebrow. 'Familiarise me with the area.'

She let out a laugh and shook her head, looking at
Regan. She moved closer to talk to him. 'Big day at
nursery?'

Regan nodded in a tired kind of way. 'It's cool,' he
whispered.

Joe gave his back a rub. 'I suspect Master Lennox is
struggling with jet-lag. Once we've eaten I think I'll get
him straight to bed.'

Lien looked up and down the street. 'What does
Regan like? Are there foods he doesn't eat? Or is he al-
lergic to anything?'

Joe gave a brief shake of his head. 'Take us somewhere you like, somewhere good. The wee man will
more or less try anything.'

Lien let out a laugh.

'What?' Joe's brow creased. 'What is it?'

Her eyes were gleaming. 'Have you any idea how Scottish you just sounded?'

She started walking down the street and he fell into step alongside her. 'Don't I always sound Scottish? I know my accent is a bit thick—'

'A bit?' Now it was her turn to raise her eyebrows.

He laughed now too. They crossed a few streets and she showed him into a small Vietnamese restaurant. By the way they greeted her it was clear she was a regular.

They sat in a booth and Regan settled next to his dad. He seemed to perk up a little. 'Are we getting food?'

'Yip,' said Joe, glancing at the menu. His smile broadened and he looked up at Lien.

She was leaning her head on one hand and watching them both. She too had a big smile on her face, and he knew exactly why.

'What's on the menu, Dad?' asked Regan.

'What's on the menu, Lien?' he asked. He nudged Regan. 'What do you want to eat tonight? I think we're going to get Lien to order for us.'

He slid the menu across the table towards Lien. It was entirely in Vietnamese. He was really going to have to get a handle on the language. He didn't even know how to order fries somewhere—the staple food of lots of kids.

'Rice and more pork,' said Regan brightly. 'And can it be a little bit spicy like the kind we had last night?'

Joe almost gave a sigh of relief. He was lucky Regan was such a great eater. With the exception of Brussels sprouts, there was very little his son would refuse.

Lien leaned across the table towards Regan. 'Oh, they do the best spicy pork in here. We can definitely get you that.' She looked up. 'What about you, Joe?'

'I'll just get the same as Regan.' He pulled a face. 'But can you order big? I'm famished—I skipped lunch.'

'You did?' She frowned and sat back. 'I thought you took a break today.'

He glanced down at his son, and mussed Regan's hair. 'I went to check on Regan. Didn't have time to eat.'

She gave him an appreciative glance, then turned to their waiter and ordered rapidly in Vietnamese for them all. As she did it, she flicked a bit of hair out of her face. He smiled. She did that often. There was always a strand that seemed to defy the ponytail band or clip she wore to tie her hair back. It was a habit, one he found endearing. He straightened in his chair. Where had that thought come from? He focused his thoughts back on his sleepy son.

She was right about the restaurant. It was a good choice. The food arrived quickly, and they chatted easily while they ate.

He could see Lien gradually beginning to relax further. The more she relaxed, the more animated she became. He started to realise just how stressed she must have been earlier by his actions. Trouble was, he really wanted to check on the family again at some point. He just wasn't sure how to do it without getting on her wrong side.

By the time they finished eating, Regan was sleepy again and Joe gathered him into his arms to carry him back to the house.

Lien smiled. 'It's getting to be a habit, isn't it? Don't worry. It takes some adults a whole week to adjust to jet-lag. Got to imagine it's worse for kids.'

They walked along the main road back to the hospital. 'Do we need to do anything when we get back?'

She shook her head. 'Dr Nguyen—Phan, you met him earlier—is on call tonight. You'll have that pleasure later in the week.'

He nodded. 'Well, since I'm only a few steps away, that seems fine.'

'There aren't many emergencies at night,' she said, her dark hair catching in the wind. 'An IV might need to be re-sited, but unless someone appears at the door, being on call is generally just about being available if needed.'

'So what do you do on your nights off, then—apart from show the best restaurants to your new colleagues?' He wasn't quite sure where that question had come from. It was out before he had much of a chance to think about it. But he was curious.

She gave him a half-smile. 'Are you being nosy, Joe?'

He dragged one hand across his brow. 'Phew. I must be at least half-forgiven. I didn't get *Dr Lennox*.'

She laughed. He could tell she was trying decide what to say. It had only been one day, but she appeared to live alone in the house next door. There had been no mention of another half. But that didn't mean she didn't have one.

'To be honest, I concentrate on work most of the time.'

There was something about the way she said those words. A hint of regret. A hint of something else.

'Not married?' What was wrong with him? His mouth seemed to be having a field day of talking before his brain could engage.

'Me? No way.' She held up one hand. 'When would I have time to be married? I spend just about every waking hour at the hospital.' Then she laughed. 'Plus the non-waking hours.' She wagged a finger at him. 'The only exception is when I have to chase after our international doctors who have crazy ideas.'

This time he made sure his brain engaged before he leapt to his own defence. 'Can we have a chat about that tomorrow? There are a few things I want to run past you.'

She rolled her eyes. 'Dr Lennox,' she said with a smile on her face, 'why do I get the impression you're going to be trouble?'

# CHAPTER THREE

THEY'D FALLEN INTO an easy routine. Joe was keen and enthusiastic, and she couldn't fault his clinical skills for a second. Which was just as well as the place was even busier than usual. Khiem and Hoa had returned for a week, and then gone to the other hospital in Uông Bí in the northeast of Vietnam.

They'd quickly given their approval of the latest employee, loving his enthusiasm and listening to his wide range of ideas.

She couldn't help but admire the relationship Joe had with his son. When they weren't working, he devoted all his time to Regan. The little boy seemed to love his new environment. He'd even tried a few Vietnamese words on Lien that he'd learned at nursery. She was impressed.

Her fears had started to settle. Even after the awkward first day, Joe didn't seem inclined to jump on the first plane back home.

Dinner at her favourite restaurant had been…interesting. His dark green eyes often had a glint of cheekiness in them, and she liked that. She was beginning to believe that he really was looking for a fresh start—even if he was only here for six months. Apart from his mum and dad, he rarely mentioned home. It was almost as if he was putting things firmly behind him. He'd been learning the language basics from Mai Ahn, and had taken an interest in some of the wider public health issues in the area.

The biggest adult health problem in Hanoi was strokes. Joe had been keen to assess every adult who attended the clinic—with any condition—to see if they were at risk. Blood-pressure medications and dietary advice were at the top of his list of general patient care. She could be annoyed. He'd started something that was in her future plans. But sometimes new blood was needed to kick-start things, so she was happy to go along with his ideas.

He'd also followed up on the family with tuberculosis. The younger two children had tested negative and been vaccinated to protect them. The father and grandfather were being actively encouraged to keep taking their medications, and the other little girl was being regularly reviewed at the clinic.

Lien stretched her hands above her head to try and relieve her aching back.

'Whoops.' Joe put his hand up to his face as he walked in the door opposite.

Heat rushed into her cheeks as she pulled her shirt back down. He'd clearly got a flash of her abdomen.

'What do you have?' she asked quickly.

'Just an adult with what could be appendicitis.' He frowned. 'I know there's a theatre here, but I'm definitely no surgeon. What do we do with patients like this?'

Her hands gave her shirt another pull and she moved over to stand next to him. 'We generally monitor for a few hours, then, if we have to, we arrange an ambulance and admission to one of the bigger hospitals.'

'How does that work for payment?'

'It's an emergency surgery and should be covered. But things can be tricky. Sometimes patients get billed for the ambulance or for the nursing care. Sometimes they get billed for nothing at all.'

She pulled the notes towards her. 'Let's see. We have a few patients with grumbling appendices. They like to wait until they absolutely have to come out.'

Joe ran his fingers through his hair in frustration. 'This guy is obviously in pain. I'll go and give him something in the meantime.' He put his hands on his hips. 'Can't you persuade someone to do free surgery for your patients?'

She smiled. 'It's on our wish list, along with free hospital care, free rehab, addiction and mental health services.'

He nodded slowly. 'I guess it's a long list, then.'

'It is.' She could tell he was feeling a bit despondent. She reached up to put her hand on his arm. 'You'll get used to the differences here. We all want to do more than we actually can.'

His eyes went to her fingers resting on his arm. He didn't say anything or pull away. He just stayed still. His gaze made her self-conscious and she stepped back, feeling a bit flustered.

'What are your plans for tomorrow?'

Joe blinked. It was as if she'd lost him for a moment. 'What?' He shook his head. 'Nothing. Just spending some time with Regan.'

'Would you like me to show you some of the sights?'

His head tilted to one side, as if he was considering the offer. She was still a little flustered and her mouth just kept talking. 'There are a few places not too far away that you might not have had a chance to visit yet. Have you been to Hoàn Kiếm Lake yet? Or Ngoc Son Temple?'

Joe shook his head. 'No. We haven't really had a chance to see much of the city. Is it something Joe would like?'

She nodded and smiled. 'Sure. It's a lake with boats and turtles. He's a kid. Of course he'll like it.'

She said it so matter-of-factly that Joe burst out laughing.

She nodded. 'Okay, then, let's finish up with this patient and see if he needs to be transferred, or if he just needs to be monitored overnight. Neither of us is on call tomorrow so we can take Regan out for the day.'

Her skin prickled. Joe was looking at her a little strangely. 'Thank you,' he said after a few seconds.

'What for?'

'For thinking about Regan.'

She shrugged. 'What are friends for?'


The next morning seemed to come around quickly. By nine o'clock they were walking to Hoàn Kiếm Lake. Even though it was a weekend morning, the lake seemed as popular with locals as it was with tourists. The large green lake was surrounded by grass and old trees. There was a whole variety of activities going on, from joggers circling the lake, to walking groups and people doing exercises beside the still water. Tourist groups with guides carrying bright umbrellas hurried around the lake shore, obviously anxious to complete this part of their tour before the sun rose too high in the sky.

Regan was excited and bounced on his toes. 'It's just like the one back home, Daddy,' he said.

Joe nodded thoughtfully. 'Maybe.' He glanced at Lien. 'There's a park we go to back home.' He paused. 'There are a lot of parks actually, but Regan's favourite is Rouken Glen. There's a lake and a gorgeous boathouse for food.' He smiled down affectionately at Regan and ruffled his hair. 'But it's not quite on this scale.' He held up one hand. 'This place seems more...elegant.'

He was struck by how many similarities he could see between Hanoi and Glasgow. It hadn't even occurred to him before he'd got here. He'd partly hoped that moving to a new place would flood him with a whole host of new emotions—leaving no time or space for new ones. It seemed he was going to have to work a little harder at leaving Glasgow behind.

'This is one of my favourite places for people-watching,' said Lien as she showed them around. 'Hoàn Kiếm Lake means "Lake of the Restored Sword".'

Regan's eyes went wide. 'Wow,' he said quickly.

She bent down next to him. 'The legend says that Emperor Lê Lợi had just won a great battle against the Ming dynasty. It was rumoured he had a magical sword that helped him win that battle. The sword was supposed to have great power and be inscribed with the words "Thuận Thiên", which means "The Will of Heaven".' She gave a broad smile. 'I think you have a similar story back in the UK about King Arthur and his sword Excalibur. Didn't he get his sword from the Lady of the Lake?'

Regan's eyes flitted to Joe's and back again. He tugged at Lien's sleeve. 'Tell me about this sword.'

She had an art for storytelling. She seemed able to pull them into the stories she was telling, putting her own special spin on them so they were suitable for Regan. 'Well, one of Lê Lợi's fishermen had found this sword. He caught the blade in his net. It was thought it had come from the Dragon King's underwater palace. Once he had the blade, Lê Lợi found the hilt—the bottom of the sword—inside a banyan tree. His soldiers said that Lê Lợi grew very tall when he used the sword and that it gave him the strength of many men.'

'Is that how he won the battle?' asked Regan eagerly.

Lien smiled and nodded. 'Lê Lợi won the battle and the Chinese accepted Vietnam as a country in its own right. Shortly after, Lê Lợi was boating on this lake—it was called Luc Thuy then, the Green Water Lake—when a golden turtle appeared. The turtle told him he'd been given the sword to protect the country against the enemy, but now it was time to return it. The turtle took the sword from Lê Lợi's belt and dived back to the bottom of the lake with the glowing sword. At first, Lê Lợi tried to find the sword as he wanted it back, but then he realised it had gone back to its rightful owner, the Dragon King.'

Regan ran to the edge and peered into the green depths. 'Do you think the sword is still down there?'

Lien grabbed his hand. She could almost see the tiny mind working. 'I think it is, but it's back with its rightful owner.'

Regan's eyes remained wide. He was staring out across the expanse of the green lake when something else caught his eye. 'Look!' He pointed.

Joe and Lien followed his gaze and saw a wedding party gathered at the other side. She nodded. 'This is a popular place to get married or to take wedding pictures. There are a few temples around here.'

'What kind of temples?'

Joe had just opened his mouth to ask the same question but Regan got there first. Joe let out a laugh. It was almost as if Lien had his son under some kind of spell. He was literally hanging on her every word. And Joe could understand why.

She was animated when she talked to him, using her hands and gestures to draw him in. Her eyes were full of fire.

'Let's go to the Ngoc Son Temple. It's on an island in the middle of the lake. We have to walk around this way.'

She guided them around the lake. Every now and then they stopped at some other sight—people doing yoga on mats, another group practising tai chi. Every time Regan spotted a ripple on the lake surface he would yell, 'Is it a turtle?'

'I wish it was,' sighed Lien. 'There are only a few left. But keep a lookout, we might spot one.'

They reached a brightly painted ornate red bridge that had a stream of people walking across it. 'This is the Huc Bridge—that means "morning sunlight". It leads us to Jade Island.'

Lien bought some tickets from a booth and they joined the crowd of people filing across the bridge. Regan kept staring expectantly into the water of the lake, hoping to spot an elusive turtle. Lien pointed further down the lake to what looked like an abandoned building on another island. 'That's the Turtle Tower. It's the place where the turtles are supposed to live and breed.' She gave a sad kind of shrug. 'Here's hoping there are still some left.'

She turned back and continued across the bridge. Joe caught his breath as the temple emerged. It was beautiful. Built in traditional Vietnamese style, it was grey in colour with splashes of white and blue.

Lien gave a smile as the people in front of them

stopped to take some photos. 'This was built in the eighteenth century and honours one of the military leaders. He fought against the Yuan Dynasty.'

Regan's brow furrowed. 'There was a lot of fighting.'

Lien knelt next to him. 'There's a lot of fighting all over the world. Thankfully this was all hundreds of years ago and we don't need to worry now.'

She turned back to the temple as they walked forward. 'It's still used—and it's been repaired a number of times over the years.' She lowered her voice as they walked through the main entrance. 'Monks pray here, and you can smell the burning incense.' She showed them around the various buildings on the small island, explaining them all. There were many antiques displayed with the temple, along with the preserved remains of a turtle that had been captured on the lake many years before.

Lien said, 'Some people think the last one died a few years ago.' She bent down and whispered in Regan's ear, 'But I live in hope that there are a few still in there, and they're hiding from all the people. I bet they come out at night.'

They spent a while on the island, taking pictures and looking at the displays. Joe could sense that Regan was starting to get distracted, and they led him back across the red bridge and back to the grounds around the lake.

They sat on the grass underneath one of the trees for a while as the sun climbed in the sky. Joe reapplied Regan's insect repellent, then Lien took them to a nearby store that sold ice cream.

They walked along the busy streets with their ice creams dripping. It was only when they stopped at one of the crossings that Joe sucked in a breath.

He hadn't thought about Esther today. Not at all.

Pain sliced through him. For a long, long time she'd been the first thing he'd thought about in the morning and the last thing he'd thought about at night.

This morning they'd just been so busy waking up and getting ready that they really hadn't had a minute. All Joe's thoughts had been on Regan and Lien.

He'd known this would happen at some point but guilt still flooded through him. He'd promised Esther he would keep her memory alive in his son, and how could he do that if he hadn't even spared her a thought today?

'Joe? What's wrong?'

Lien was standing in front of him, her nose only inches below his, chocolate ice cream dripping down her hand.

He jerked back. 'What?' He felt a bit confused.

She gave him a curious smile and he noticed she was holding Regan's hand. 'The lights changed for us to cross, and you missed them. We had to come back for you.'

He flinched. Had he really been so lost in his own thoughts? Heat rushed into his cheeks. Not only was he embarrassed, he was angry with himself. What if something had happened to Regan?

He noticed the crossing lights change again behind Lien's head. 'Let's go,' she said easily, as if nothing had happened.

He sucked in a breath as he watched her slim figure in white loose trousers and a bright pink long-sleeved tunic walk in front of him. From the way the sun was striking her, he could see the outline of her body beneath the thin clothes.

They'd taken a hundred photos today. Some together, and some of just Regan and Lien.

He licked his lips as he tried to rationalise the blood racing around his body. She was good for him. She was good for them.

Of course, she was a colleague. It was quite likely she had a no-date rule for work. And that was fine. Because he had to deal with his feelings before he could even consider anything else.

This was the first time he'd felt this rush, this attraction, in for ever. At least it felt like for ever.

The only woman Regan had really had in his life since Esther had died had been Joe's mother, and while she was great, it was nice to see him interact so well with someone else. He watched as they stopped at the other side of the street and Lien pulled some tissues from her bag so they could all wipe their sticky fingers.

She looked over the top of Regan's head. 'You okay?' she asked softly.

It was almost like she knew. As if she'd read his mind.

His heart stuttered, partly because of the empathy she showed and partly from the thought that if she *could* read his mind, she might not be entirely happy with some of the thoughts he'd been having.

He gave a quick nod of his head. 'I'm fine.'

He sucked a deep breath in and closed his eyes for a second, inhaling the scent from the nearby street vendor carts. As he opened his eyes again he took in the bright splashes of colour all around them, and his ears adjusted to the constant buzz of noise. He smiled. Vietnam. Something about this city was giving him a new lease on life.

* * *

The next two days were busy. No time to sightsee or do anything other than work. Lien liked that. It was normal for her. But she was conscious of the fact that Joe was used to more support back home. She also wondered how well he was sleeping. She'd noticed some dark circles under his eyes today. Her hand paused at the blue door, wondering if she should knock or not. She wasn't being nosy but she hadn't seen Regan for a few days.

From the smell wafting through the open window she could tell they'd already had dinner. Good. She wouldn't be interrupting. She knocked at the door and pushed it open when she heard the shout telling her to enter.

Joe waved her inside. Regan was perched on the edge of the sofa and she could see they had an electronic tablet in their hands. 'We're just video-calling back home with my mum and dad,' he explained. He moved over on the sofa. 'Come and say hello.'

She shook her head quickly and backed up. 'Sorry, I didn't mean to interrupt.'

'Don't go.' He smiled and waved his hand, beckoning her inside. 'Come. My mum and dad want to say hello.'

She smiled nervously. This definitely felt like an intrusion, but Regan waved her over too. 'Come on, Lien, say hi to my grandma.'

Lien took a few steps and sat down nervously next to Joe. There was an older couple on the screen, waving at her.

'Mum, Dad, this is Lien.'

Regan stuck his head across the screen. 'She works with Daddy.'

Joe nodded to the screen. 'Lien, this is Rob and Ann, my mum and dad.'

Lien laughed nervously and waved back.

The woman, Ann, stepped right up to the screen, obviously to get a better look at her. She clasped her hands together. 'Lien, it's so nice to meet you. Regan's been talking about you and how you live in the house next door.'

Lien nodded. 'Yes, that's right. I'm next door.'

She'd spent her life talking to patients and relatives— usually complete strangers—and managed perfectly well. But right now she'd never felt so awkward. She had the strangest sensation of meeting a boyfriend's mum when she was nineteen years old, and vowing not to set foot in that house again.

His mum had been nice, but it was clear she didn't think anyone would be good enough for her son.

Ann kept talking. 'How are they getting on? Regan says he likes the nursery, have you seen it? Does it have a good reputation? And Joe? Is he behaving? And how big is the laundry pile? Has he started wearing crumpled shirts yet?'

Lien's head was buzzing, not least with the speed of the barrage of questions, but also with the broad Scottish accents. She actually started laughing.

Joe gave a casual shrug and rolled his eyes. 'See, Regan? I told you. She doesn't believe a word we say.' He gave Lien a slight nudge. 'Go on, back me up here.'

She turned from Joe to Regan and back to Ann. Rob stood in the background with his arms folded and his head shaking in amusement. It was clear he was used to all this.

Lien started to brush off the nerves. She shook her head. 'Oh, no. I know how this works. I'm Team Ann.'

Joe's mother's face broke into a wide grin and the

older woman held up her hand towards the screen. 'High five!' she said.

Lien returned the gesture. 'High five.' She shifted on the sofa. 'So, the real story is, yes, your boys are doing fine. The nursery is great and Regan...' she gave the boy an appreciative nod '...is mastering the language better than his dad.' She gave Joe a quick glance. 'As for Joe, well...' she put her hand to her face '...where do I start?'

Ann started laughing and Joe leaned forward. He gave Lien a pretend shocked look. 'What? No way?'

Lien shrugged. 'Well, he seems to be doing okay in the doctor department but sometimes...' she gave a slow nod and an amused grin '...he needs to be reined in.'

'Oh, don't I know it!' declared Ann.

Lien pretended to look over the back of the sofa. 'As for the laundry basket... I wouldn't like to comment.'

Regan was laughing so hard he fell off the edge of the sofa and jumped back up again almost instantaneously. All four adults let out a yelp at once, and then a sigh of relief.

This time Rob stepped forward. He exchanged glances with his wife and put an arm around her waist. 'We're so glad to meet you, Lien,' he said. She could see the genuine appreciation in his eyes. 'We're relieved there's someone to keep an eye on our boys.'

Something panged inside her. They missed Joe and Regan. It was obvious. But there was something else too. Joe had told her that his mother had pushed him in this direction. She could almost see the older couple reaching through the screen and making a grab for the hopefulness they could see. She suddenly realised how this must look.

'Everyone at the hospital is looking out for them,' she said quickly.

Ann still had her gaze fixed on Lien, who tried not to look nervous, or shift uncomfortably. She didn't want his mum and dad getting the wrong idea. She reached a hand out and patted Joe's leg. 'I'll leave you to it,' she said, as she stood up.

Joe gave her a strange look, his gaze fixing on her hand. Of course. She'd just touched his leg. It had been an unwitting move. There had been no intent. But she doubted she'd helped things.

She gave her head a tiny shake and shot him a look of apology. 'Nice to meet you, Rob and Ann.' She waved at the screen as Regan climbed onto her vacated spot on the sofa.

She reached the door and glanced back. Regan had started talking again quickly, regaling his grandparents with stories from the nursery. But Joe's eyes were fixed on hers.

She couldn't quite tell what the expression on his face meant. Was he angry at her? Annoyed? No.

It was almost like…something else. As if a veil had just lifted from his eyes and he was seeing her in a different light.

The tiny hairs on her arms stood on end as her skin prickled instantly. She lifted her hand in a silent wave and ducked out the door, crossing the ground to her own house in double quick time.

When she opened her own door she closed it firmly behind her and stood for a second, leaning against it. What was wrong with her? Nothing had happened. Nothing had been said. But every cell in her body was on red alert. Her heart was racing. And somehow she knew it wasn't from her burst of quick walking.

But there was something else. Something more subconscious. His parents were lovely, and clearly good fun. But she'd noticed something. It couldn't be helped. It was obvious.

They'd been in the garden of their home. Their very *large* home. She had no idea about how people lived in Scotland, but she could tell a very large home and beautiful gardens at first glance. It all meant money. Joe's family was rich. And she had experience of rich families.

Her stomach twisted uncomfortably. There was obviously something wrong with her. Why had those thoughts even come into her head? Joe was only a work colleague. Nothing else. She was merely being hospitable.

But if she was only being hospitable, why did the fact he had a rich family back in Scotland make her want to run in the opposite direction?

She closed her eyes for a second and leaned her head back. This was crazy. *She* was crazy. She just wasn't quite sure what came next.

Regan was oblivious to the subtleties of adults. He took every question about Lien at face value and blurted out answers left, right and centre.

Joe sat quietly cringing. The only thing was, he couldn't help but smile. He could read his mum and dad like a book and shook his head at a few of their more inquisitive comments, pretending he hadn't even heard them.

Eventually, he grabbed Regan and pulled him onto

his lap. 'Say goodnight to Grandma and Papa. It's time for bed.'

His mother pulled a face and started to blow kisses. Then, just as they were about to disconnect, his father shot in a quick comment. 'Love to Lien!'

Joe was sure the second the connection ended they'd be hugging each other. He spent the next half-hour settling Regan into bed and making up some story about pirates, before making his way back to turn out the lights. 'Not as good as Lien,' Regan murmured in a sleepy voice.

Joe left the room smiling and glanced out of the window. The pale lilac door was taunting him. Begging him to knock on it.

None of this had been planned. When Lien had appeared at the door it had seemed only natural to call her over to say hello to his parents. He'd half hoped it might give them some reassurance that he and Regan had actually settled in.

Instead, it had opened a whole new can of worms.

He felt his phone buzz and pulled it from his pocket. A text from his mother. Three words.

We love her.

Nothing else.

Guilt swamped him. What was he doing? As soon as Lien had sat down she'd fallen into the family conversation with no problems and been an instant hit with his parents.

He couldn't pretend that hadn't pleased him. He'd liked the way they'd exchanged glances of approval and joked and laughed with her.

But it also—in a completely strange way—*didn't* please him.

Part of him still belonged to Esther. Always had. Always would.

He'd found love once. He'd been lucky. Some people would never have what he and Esther had.

How dared he even contemplate looking again?

His mother had pushed him here to start living again. Not to find a replacement for his wife.

The thought made his legs crumple and he slid down the wall, his hands going to his hair. For a few seconds he just breathed.

He was pulling himself one way and another. Guilt hung over him like a heavy cloud.

He knew why he was here. He knew he'd been living life back in Scotland in a protective bubble. It *was* time to get out there. That was why he'd accepted the tickets and climbed on that plane.

But what he hated most of all was that he did feel ready to move on. He was tired. He was tired of being Joe the widower. It had started to feel like a placard above his head.

But part of him hated the fact he wanted to move forward. He was tired of being alone. He was tired of feeling like there would never by anyone else in his and Regan's lives. He was tired of being tired. Of course, he had no idea about the kind of person he was interested in. The truth was, the few little moments that Lien had caused sparks in his brain had bothered him.

It had been so long and he couldn't quite work out how he felt about everything yet. Of course he'd want someone who recognised that he and Regan were a package deal. He'd want someone who could understand his usual passion for this work. These last few weeks had mirrored how he'd been a few years before. Every day there was something new to learn. Someone new to help. It was what had always driven him, and he knew that, for a while, he'd lost that. But Vietnam was reawakening parts of him that had been sleeping for a while.

He lifted his head and peeled his damp shirt from his back and sighed. Too much thinking wasn't good for a man.

# CHAPTER FOUR

LIEN FINISHED WRITING up the notes on her last patient just as one of the nurses stuck her head around the door. 'Lien? I know it's late, but Joe asked if you'd mind dropping in at his house on the way home. There's something he wants to talk to you about.'

She couldn't help the way her face automatically curved into a smile. It seemed the nurse noticed too as she gave Lien an amused glance. 'Okay, then, see you later.'

Lien glanced at her watch. It was late. Regan would likely be sleeping by now. She couldn't help but be curious. What did Joe want to talk to her about?

She washed her hands and pulled her shirt a little straighter, then walked across the grounds towards his blue door.

She knocked lightly, waiting for only a second before he pulled it open with a tired smile. 'Come in.'

He was wearing a white T-shirt and some lightweight jogging trousers. From the way he had papers scattered across the table he'd been working on this for some time.

He gestured towards the table, indicating she should sit next to him. In the last few weeks he'd made this place a bit homier. There were now a few pictures scattered around, and it looked like he'd finally got around to buying a laundry basket to get on top of the washing. She could see a haphazardly folded pile of clean clothes sitting on a chair in the corner of the room.

'Want something to eat?'

She shook her head. She'd been hungry a few hours ago, but the feeling had passed. He held up a tin that she knew was where he kept Regan's favourite biscuits. 'One of these?'

'Go on, then,' she said. 'But promise not to tell him.'

Joe smiled. 'Oh, too late, he has these counted. I'll need to account for the missing biscuit tomorrow.'

She bit into the chocolate-coated biscuit. It was one that Regan's grandparents sent every few weeks from Scotland and she was beginning to think she was getting quietly addicted to them.

There was a noise, a bit like a whimper, and Joe crossed to Regan's doorway. As she watched she could sense his breathing get heavier. It was clear he had something on his mind. She waited a few moments, and when he didn't move, she crossed over to stand just behind his shoulder.

Regan was curled into a little ball. His lips were moving, as if he were singing some song or nursery rhyme in his sleep.

Joe took a deep breath, his voice so low it was barely a whisper, his eyes fixed on Regan.

'Sometimes when I'm in my bed at night, I get up and watch Regan sleeping. Then I start to wonder, is there some horrible, secret gene that predisposes you to cancer?'

Lien's stomach gave an uncomfortable twist. He kept talking, his voice racked with emotion.

'Both of Esther's parents died of different types of cancer, and she died of leukaemia. So I look at my little boy and wonder if there's even a tiny possibility that he might have inherited something that I don't know about, can't see, and won't find out about until it smacks us in the face.' His voice was shaking now, as were his hands.

She slid her arm through his.

He shook his head. 'I know it's crazy. I know it's irrational. But I can't help it.'

Her voice was tinged with sadness because she got the impression he'd been hiding these feelings for a while, storing them up, letting them fester, and not sharing them with anyone else. 'But it's not irrational, and it's not crazy, Joe. It's the thoughts of a man who has already lost his wife, and is terrified he might lose his son.'

She hated the fact they were having this conversation. She could reach out and touch his pain. It was so visible in the air it was practically creating a cloud around his head.

There was also a tiny twinge in her that wondered if this was why he'd asked her here. She'd been bright and happy about the invitation, hoping that—just maybe—it was for something other than work.

But now he was talking to her about his dead wife, and his fears for his son. Her heart ached for him, but she was also trying hard to hide the tinge of disappointment she felt.

She should have been pleased that he felt he could reveal this part of himself to her. But somehow it also gave her the feeling that, no matter what Joe said out loud, his heart really wasn't ready to move on.

She ran her fingertips along his bare skin. 'I can't say much to help, because we do know some cancers seem to run in families. But think back. Think back to the random patients you've seen over the years that came in with symptoms. Symptoms that led to a diagnosis of...' she paused for a second, obviously recalling a few cases '...skin cancer, anal cancer, prostate cancer or renal cancer. People with no family history at all. It happens all the time.'

She stopped talking for a few minutes and just let him consider. 'Sometimes it's easier to see the things that worry us most.' She paused and gave him a sympathetic smile. 'The kinds of things that keep you awake in your bed at night.'

'What kind of doctor does that make me then?' He looked pained.

She shook her head. 'No kind of doctor. Just a worried parent. You don't have to be a doctor every moment of your life, Joe.' She looked up into his worried green eyes and gave him the softest smile. They were barely inches apart now. 'Make room for other things,' she whispered.

It was almost as if she'd touched a nerve. He jerked. He physically jerked at the impact of her words and she immediately averted her eyes, embarrassed for them both. She moved back quickly to the table and sat down, giving him a few moments to join her.

Her brain was whirring now. She shouldn't have touched him. How could she explain that it had been done in empathy for how he was feeling?

She wasn't really that surprised that he was feeling vulnerable right now. He was in a strange country with his son. Yes, they seemed to have settled well, but who really knew what went on inside someone else's mind?

Clearly not her. No matter how much she tried to deny it, she was beginning to feel a connection to this guy.

But after that reaction she was apparently not reading things well. She'd just embarrassed them both. The easiest thing to do was try to pretend nothing had happened.

She shifted a little in the seat. The last thing she wanted to do was sit here in his company after that.

But she still had to work with this guy every day. So she took a deep breath and plastered an interested look on her face, ignoring the little strands of hurt she felt inside.

His phone buzzed with a text and when it flashed up, she saw the screenshot that lay behind it. It was the same photo that Regan had next to his bed. The picture of Esther on the beach, laughing.

Something twisted inside her. She had no reason to be jealous, absolutely none. Of course Regan should have a picture of his mum, but did Joe also need to have it on his phone?

She stared at the array of papers alongside a laptop on the table. 'What on earth have you been doing?'

As he sat down at the table and started organising his papers her eyes went to one of the pictures Joe had put on the wall. What drew her attention was a large, grand-looking house surrounded by an expanse of gardens. From the view and setting it seemed to be back in Scotland. Joe and Regan were standing in front of the property—it was clearly their family home. She had no idea what house prices were like over there, but one look at the obviously expensive property made her feel distinctly uncomfortable. She'd already seen the house belonging to Joe's mum and dad, but this must be the house that Joe and Regan lived in. She tried not to calculate in her head how many times this tiny two-bed bungalow could fit into that grand house. What was the English

TV series set before the war, where they had staff? It was nearly as big as that.

'Is that a house or a castle?' she quipped. Unease spread across her. No, more than that. It was like every nerve in her body was on edge; she could sense the instant hostility and she couldn't do a darned thing about it. It was like every automatic defence system had just slid into place.

'It's not a castle,' he said with a wave of his hand, then peered back at the screen. 'At least, I don't think it was.'

Her skin prickled. She actually wasn't sure if he was joking or not. She licked her lips. It was funny how being uncomfortable made her mouth instantly dry. 'Bigger than the average house, I imagine.' She tried to make her voice sound casual.

He leaned back against the sofa and nodded towards the window and the hospital across from them. 'Not as big as this place.'

She folded her arms across her chest. 'I'm not so sure.'

He shook his head. 'Nah,' he said breezily. 'And anyway, didn't you know everyone lives in a castle in Scotland?'

Of course he was joking, but just the way he said those words tugged at something inside her, and not in a good way. History had taught her that only those who had never had to worry about money would make a quip like that.

'Here.' He turned a large piece of paper around to face her. He hadn't thought twice about their conversation. He hadn't even noticed her reaction.

She bent forward. It was a map of the surrounding areas. It was littered with red and blue dots.

'What is this?' She was confused.

'I decided to take a look at some of our patients,' he said. His fingers traced across the paper. 'The ones with the red dots are the patients currently attending that have tuberculosis. The ones with blue dots are the ones we know have multi-resistant tuberculosis.' He leaned forward so his head was almost touching hers. 'Look here. This is the biggest cluster.'

She nodded slowly. The information wasn't a surprise to her, she'd just never seen it laid out this way. Her skin prickled. The district with the biggest incidence of tuberculosis was the one where her parents lived, and in which she'd been brought up.

He kept talking as he moved some papers around the desk. 'Okay, so you don't like me going out and doing follow-ups...' he gave her a slightly teasing smile '...but I got to thinking. I've checked up on some of these patients. There's a low uptake of tuberculosis vaccinations after birth. Not everyone is bringing their children to the clinic. What about if we set up a kind of pop-up clinic to try and screen some people for TB, and immunise any kids that have been missed?'

He was clearly brimming with enthusiasm at the prospect. 'Is this district one I should be worried about? Are the crime rates high there?' He kept talking without waiting for a response. 'Because I've checked some of the other stats. I know there's deprivation and poor health. I know one of the biggest issues for the kids in that area is malnutrition. Maybe we could try and do something to address that while we're there?'

Something swept over her. Resentment. A wave of anger. 'What, do you want to give them all money to feed their kids too?'

He pulled back, obviously surprised by her outburst.

She ran her fingers through her hair. 'Do you think we haven't tried these things before?' she asked. 'Do you think we haven't tried to find new ways to help the people who need it most?' Her words came out more fiercely than she'd meant them to, but she couldn't hide how many buttons his ideas had just pushed.

Joe was looking at her with cautious eyes. He clasped both hands together and spoke carefully. 'Of course I think you've tried different things. But sometimes it's a timing issue. All I'm saying is maybe it's time to try again.' His voice was low. 'I don't know the people in these areas the way that the rest of the staff here do. I can only look from an outside point of view. My public health head tells me we have a current hotspot for tuberculosis, and potentially more cases of multi-resistance. Can't we take a look at this?'

He spoke so earnestly she knew he meant every word of this. She couldn't help but be oversensitive. She often felt like this when outsiders remarked on the area she'd been brought up in. People made so many judgements. Formed so many opinions.

She struggled to find the right words. 'Let me think about it. We can discuss it with Khiem and Hoa. Setting up pop-up clinics is more difficult than it sounds.'

Joe pressed his lips together and ran his fingers through his hair. She could tell he was frustrated. He'd probably wanted her to jump all over his idea and tell him it was wonderful. And in some ways it probably was.

He leaned back and stretched his arms out. 'Regan is hankering after another bedtime story from you. He'll be sorry he missed you tonight.'

'Couldn't be helped,' she said as lightly as she could.

'We can catch up some other time.' She gave Joe a softer look. 'Are your stories really that bad?'

He smiled. 'Not bad. Just the same. I keep recycling, and Regan's now getting old enough to realise that.' He raised his eyebrows. 'Whereas you swept in here with your dragons, warriors and magic turtles and blew me out of the water.'

She raised her eyebrows in challenge. 'Time to up your game, then.'

He shook his head. 'Oh, no way. I'm not getting into that. You have an unfair advantage.'

'What's that?' The atmosphere between them was definitely mellowing. She was starting to calm down. Gain a bit of perspective. She'd had no reason to act so hurt about earlier. He'd clearly been sad, vulnerable and worried about his child. Over-reacting wouldn't do either of them any good.

He waved his hand. 'Untried and untested kids' stories.'

'Who says they're untried and untested? I've worked the children's clinic for a while now. It's amazing what you can learn when you start telling a chid a story.'

His face changed, becoming more serious, and he nodded. 'Yeah, sometimes they tell you a story back that makes you want to wrap your arms around them and hide them away.'

Their gazes clashed. Unspoken words. Joe had worked as a general practitioner in Scotland for years. Doubtless he'd encountered child protection issues just like she had here. It was a sobering thought, and she didn't want to go there.

'Have you and Regan video-called with your parents again?'

He nodded. 'Oh, yes. Every Tuesday and Friday. My parents are creatures of habit. If they don't get their Regan fix they get very testy.'

'They must miss him.'

He gave a little sigh. 'Yeah, they do. And he misses them. I don't think he quite understands the distance. He's asked a few times if we can go and see them. He was used to seeing them every day, so it's a big difference.'

'You must miss them too.'

Joe paused for a second. 'I do. They've been my biggest supporters for the last few years. I don't know what I would have done if they hadn't been there when...' His voice drifted off and she filled in the blanks by herself. She didn't need him to say any more. He looked up. 'They keep asking for you too. You'll need to come and say hello again sometime.'

She smiled nervously. Something in the air felt quite odd between them. They were working together so well, and she enjoyed his company. Maybe that was it? She was enjoying his company a bit more than any other colleague's. Maybe that was why she was being so defensive? Self-protect mode kicked in when anything felt remotely personal. She wanted to keep herself safe. And how did you keep your heart safe when there was already an adorable kid tugging away at it, and a guy with the sexiest accent in the world breathing the same air?

He reached over for the biscuit tin again, offering it to her. 'Hey, you've met my mum and dad now. When do we get to meet yours? I'm sure Regan would love to say hello.'

The words came like a bolt out of the blue. It felt like a tidal wave sweeping the ground from beneath her feet.

She wasn't prepared. She wasn't ready. She swallowed. 'I...I...' Panic flooded her. This wasn't her. She was a professional. She'd had lots of questions or statements thrown at her over the years. None had made her as tongue-tied as this simple request.

She stood up quickly, scattering some of the papers that were on the table to the floor. 'Sorry,' she said. 'I've just remembered there's something I need to do.' She crossed the room quickly and opened the door, her mouth achingly dry. 'See you tomorrow.'

The thudding of her heart echoed in her ears as she hurried to her own front door. She'd seen the look on Joe's face. He'd been totally confused by her actions. But the thought of taking him to meet her parents made her stomach churn in a way she couldn't put into words.

She'd been down this road before. At medical school she'd known how to dress—designer classics bought from charity shops, clothes that had barely aged from season to season. She had been polite. She'd been able to talk about a vast range of international topics. She'd read widely. All things to hide her background from her fellow students. It had all gone so nicely. Until she'd started dating Reuben.

And he'd wanted to meet her parents. They hadn't even got that far. As soon as he'd heard where she lived, she'd been dropped like a hot brick. The look of disdain and disappointment that he'd given her had seared into her heart, destroying a little part of her for ever. It seemed as if Joe, despite his humble nature, was from just as rich a family as Reuben had been.

The thought filled her with dread. They were just colleagues, that was all.

But how could Joe meet her parents without judging

them? Wasn't that what everyone from wealth and privilege did? She didn't want that for her parents. She loved them dearly, and supported the fact they liked where they lived. But anyone walking into the neighbourhood could see the poverty there. It reached out and grabbed you from every faded awning and tumbled litter bin that was strewn across the streets. From the patched-up windows, along with the thin, angular frames of the people who lived there. Malnutrition was a big issue. Overcrowding another.

The area was home to her. Even if it wasn't the nicest area. She could name most of the families in the same street as her mother and father. Some of these people had cleaned up her grazed knees or wiped her nose when she'd been a tiny kid. She'd been invited to sit at the table of bigger families with a large bowl of food shared out between however many faces were round the table at the time. Sometimes it meant only a few spoonfuls each, but the laughter and chatter around the table had meant that bellies had felt a little less empty.

The thought of walking Joe—the man who practically lived in a castle back in Scotland—down those streets filled her with dread.

Her parents were every bit as polite and hospitable as Joe's were, and Joe didn't seem like Reuben in any other way.

But she couldn't take that chance.

She wouldn't have her parents judged the way she had been.

Not ever.

# CHAPTER FIVE

THEY SETTLED INTO an easy routine. Joe took Regan to
the international nursery every morning and was back
at the clinic to start at eight. Khiem and Hoa were back
from their other hospital, and they all split the hospital
and clinic duties between them. Joe occasionally helped
out Hoa with the maternity side of things to try and keep
his skills up. He found the friendly doctor a real pleasure
to work with, particularly around maternal conditions
and complications specific to Vietnam.

Khiem wore a different-coloured bow-tie every day
along with a long-sleeved shirt. At times Joe wondered
how he could stand the heat. After wearing shirts for the
first two months, he'd eventually adopted the same clothing as Lien and started wearing the lightweight long-
sleeved loose tunic tops that she preferred. The first time
she'd spotted him wearing a yellow one she'd laughed
and taken him to the shop that she favoured where he'd
stocked up on white, beige and pale blue versions.

He'd just finished covering the ward round when
Khiem called them all down to a staff meeting.

'How was it?' asked Lien, and he walked into the
room and sat down next to her.

'Not bad. Two chronic chests, one forty-five-year-old with a suspected stroke, and another young woman I think might have renal problems.' He shook his head. 'She hasn't admitted it but I suspect she might have tried some of the locally brewed alcohol.'

Lien screwed up her face. 'Oh, no.'

He smiled. He liked it when she did that. It was cute. Not a word he'd usually use to describe a colleague, but cute none the less. He still hadn't figured out what had made her virtually bolt from his room the other night.

But it had also been the first time since he'd arrived in Vietnam that he'd been feeling a bit worried, a bit sentimental. He had no idea why. But crazy thoughts about genetics and biology had blossomed in his mind like a tiny flower, and it hadn't helped that the flower had rapidly turned into an orchard with messy unknown things growing there. Then Lien had said a few things to reassure him he wasn't going mad.

Oh.

That.

Had she thought…? Was that why she'd seemed so off later?

Was he really so turned off to the feelings of those around him? It was hardly an admirable trait for a doctor.

'Joe?'

Lien was looking at him, and he realised he'd been part way through a conversation about a patient.

He nodded. 'Oh, yes. I've run some blood tests this morning, so when I get the results this afternoon I'll go back and ask her some more questions. I think she was being careful what she told me this morning. That, and she was just feeling so bad. She was really dehydrated so I've got her up on an IV at the moment.'

Lien sighed. 'Is she a tourist?'

He nodded. 'She's a student from Australia.'

Lien gave another sigh. 'What do you suspect—rice wine? People just don't realise how strong it is over here.' She rolled her eyes. 'The normal rice wine is bad enough, at twenty-nine per cent, but if she's drunk something unbranded...' She shook her head. 'The methanol levels can be so high they can be fatal.'

He nodded. 'I'm watching her. She's conscious. She does have abdominal pain and vomiting, but her co-ordination seems fine.'

'Any problems with her vision?'

'Not so far, but, like I said, I'm going to keep an eye on her. Right now I'll keep her hydrated and consider some bicarbonate, or maybe even some fomepizole if it's appropriate.'

She slid him a curious sideways glance. He smiled. 'Okay, you got me. I might have consulted with Khiem. It's my first potential methanol poisoning.'

She held out both hands. 'Hey, and you've been here, what, more than two months? That's almost unheard of.' She dropped her hands and gave a small shrug. 'I like it that you ask if you're not sure. She could easily have been misdiagnosed. Missing methanol poisoning can be the biggest error a physician makes around here.'

He leaned back in the chair. 'I just hope she's going to be okay. That this will just turn out to be rice wine that was too strong for her and it feels like the worst hangover in the world. Hopefully she'll recover and everything will be okay.'

Khiem hurried into the room. His wife, Hoa, came in behind him, along with a few of the other staff members. They settled down and Khiem picked up a chart from his desk. 'Sorry to keep you all. I promise this won't take long. I just wanted to let you all know that we have another staff member joining us for a month. A volunteer.'

One of the nurses frowned. 'Who is it?'

Lien shot Joe a look. She'd told him that they occasionally had volunteer doctors—usually private, very well-paid consultants who wanted to say they had at least spent some time working in the underprivileged areas in the city.

Khiem smiled brightly. 'His name is Reuben Le Gran. His father is French, his mother Vietnamese, and even though he doesn't sound it, he's a local boy. Did his training in Hanoi, and has also worked in Paris and London. He specialises in plastic surgery, and works out of a private clinic in the Tay Ho district.'

The nurse next to Joe quipped, 'Just what we need—a plastic surgeon. Bet he lives in one of the gated communities in Tay Ho.'

Joe had learned a little more about the city. He knew Tay Ho was one of the richest areas, and he'd passed by the gated communities on more than one occasion. Saying that they were opulent didn't even come close to the truth. They had twenty-four-hour security guards, private schools, golf courses and the biggest houses he'd seen in a long time.

Khiem waved his hand. 'A plastic surgeon will be good. We have lots of patients on whom he might be able to do minor procedures. We've used the mini-theatre at the back on a number of occasions. This time will be no different.' He smiled. 'He'll only be here one day a week.'

Joe turned to his other side and jolted. Lien's face was frozen and her body stiff. He could see the tense muscles at the base of her throat. Her fingers were clenching her legs. He reached over to touch her to ask what was wrong, but she jumped up.

Khiem looked surprised but just continued speaking in his jovial manner. 'And you two, Lien and Joe, there's a special request for you to go to Uông Bí to cover holiday leave at the clinic there next week.'

For a few seconds Joe wondered if Lien had heard the words, but then her face changed and she gave the briefest of nods. 'Perfect,' she said as she walked out the door.

She couldn't hide her anger. Her skin had prickled, almost like a premonition before Khiem had said the name out loud. No one here knew about her previous relationship with Reuben. Once he'd found out where she lived he hadn't exactly wanted the world to know about their connection. Reuben was the type of guy who wanted to move in the right circles and be seen with the 'in' crowd. Lien would never be one of those people.

Even if the others had known about her past relationship, she wouldn't expect them to turn down the services of a free plastic surgeon. She could think of a few patients straight off the top of her head who could really benefit from seeing him. As angry as she was at him for turning up at *her* hospital, she could be rational enough to put the needs of the patients first.

She stalked down the corridor and into the nearest bathroom, closing the door behind her and splashing some water on her face, then she rested her hands at the side of the sink and just breathed.

This wasn't an accident. Reuben was far too calculating for that. She'd tried to ignore him over the last few years, but his reputation had grown and grown, and his publicity machine had been working overtime.

His beaming face had adorned countless magazine covers as he'd become known as the 'plastic surgeon to the stars'. There was much speculation about who he'd worked on. Hollywood film stars, a top British model, three Bollywood stars and numerous other celebrities had been seen on his arm, or in his company, over the last few years. It seemed deliberate. Every time things quietened down he would whirl along some pavement with some new star and the press would go mad again. The latest rumour involved politicians, a few of whom seemed to have reversed the aging process.

Then there had been the interview given by a co-worker that had been slightly malicious. Even Lien had felt uncomfortable at its contents. Sad thing was, the words the co-worker had used about Reuben's ego being larger than his clinic, his apparent self interest, and his lack of philanthropy, had caused Vietnam's golden boy to lose a little of his shine. And Lien knew it was all entirely true.

Helping at the hospital in one of the most deprived areas in Hanoi was a prediction she could have made herself. It had been inevitable. Reuben needed some good press again. She was sure he would sweep in here with a whole host of his own staff, plus camera crew, and perform a few minor surgeries to try to claw back some of his golden-boy image.

She stared at her reflection in the mirror for a few seconds. Pressing her lips together, she straightened her shoulders.

Last time around he'd made her feel small and worthless, all because of her address. She was older now, wiser. She'd worked hard to serve the people who lived here. She'd done a good job.

The last thing she wanted was to come face to face with the smug surgeon again.

She dabbed her face dry with a paper towel and walked back to Khiem's office. Everyone else had already left. Khiem was sitting behind his desk.

'I've had some thoughts,' she said determinedly. 'Let's draw up a list of patients for our visiting surgeon.'

She didn't need to see him. She didn't need to be involved in anything that he did here. But she wanted to be sure she'd served the needs of her patients.

Khiem looked up and smiled, nodding his head. 'What a good idea.' He pulled his chair closer to Lien's. 'Let's make a start.'

# CHAPTER SIX

JOE COULD TELL something was off. Lien had been stilted this week. Not her usual relaxed self. Even Regan had noticed. 'Where's Lien? I want another dragon story,' he'd said as Joe had tucked him into bed the night before.

'Sorry, pal,' he'd sighed. 'I guess she's just busy with work.'

But as he watched her the next day, it seemed like anything but work that was on her mind. She was distracted. Tense.

The nurses had to repeat things to her on a number of occasions, and her gaze kept wandering to the main door.

He couldn't pretend he hadn't noticed her reaction the other day. Did she know this other doctor? If she did, it was clear she wasn't enamoured with him.

He'd just finished up immunising a few children when the main door opened and a guy swept in wearing a white doctor's coat.

Joe frowned in confusion, then tried not to laugh out loud. Really? No one here wore a white coat, and yet this guy had walked in off the street in one?

The door was still open, and Joe could see the black limousine parked in the street outside.

The guy smiled. 'I'm here,' he said loudly to no one in

particular. 'Reuben Le Gran, at your service.' He started striding through the clinic, his head flicking from side to side. 'Now, what do we have here?'

Joe stuck his hands in his pockets and wandered after the guy. A few people—obviously his staff—had followed him inside the clinic, most of them carrying large boxes.

Joe shook his head and walked over to the nearest woman and held out his arms. 'Let me help you.'

After a few moments Hoa appeared. Her smile was broad and she extended her hand towards the doctor. 'Reuben, it's a pleasure to meet you.'

Reuben Le Gran was taller than average for Vietnam, with broad shoulders, extremely straight white teeth and light brown skin. His thick dark hair was a slightly strange colour. Was it dyed?

Joe showed the staff through to the small theatre at the back of the hospital. He didn't even get a chance to make any introductions before the staff looked around and started speaking rapidly to each other. It seemed they were a finely honed and confident team. There was also a hint of arrogance about them that made him a bit uncomfortable. They didn't seem interested in any of the existing hospital staff, as they moved things around and set up their own equipment without a single question about whether it was convenient.

Joe could see the baffled expressions on a few of his colleagues' faces. Good. It wasn't just him. It struck him just how discourteous Reuben and his team were being. He watched the initial welcome from Hoa—one of the nicest women he'd ever met. Reuben wasn't particularly interested in her either, just immediately started talking about himself and his plans. He'd arranged to be interviewed by a TV journalist while he was working here. What was most interesting was that he seemed to favour talking in English rather than his native Vietnamese. Joe found it strange.

The dazzling white teeth were even stranger, faker than the latest TV pop star who was apparently plucked from a pavement, even though she'd clearly had every plastic surgery known to man.

Joe shook his head and took himself back off to the patients he was looking after. He wasn't interested in meeting Reuben, and it seemed Reuben wasn't interested in meeting him.

He'd only taken a few steps when he heard the words, 'Oh, you have a doctor here—Dang Van Lien. Is she on duty?'

Joe's footsteps seemed to freeze in mid-air. He sucked in a breath as he waited for Hoa's reply. 'Yes, Lien works here. Has for years. She's one of our finest doctors.'

'Yes, I'm sure she is. Can you tell her I'm looking for her?'

It was almost like a summons. Something flashed across Hoa's face. Joe had only ever seen her in friendly mode, but he had heard a few tales that she wasn't a woman to be messed with.

'Tell her yourself,' replied Hoa dryly. 'Now, take a seat please, Dr Le Gran, and we'll discuss the patients you will be seeing here.' It was as if a switch had been flicked. Ice dripped from her voice.

There was a pregnant pause.

Joe held his breath, waiting to see what the response would be. He heard the scraping of a chair. 'Of course.'

Hoa continued, 'And just so we're clear, Dr Le Gran, I make decisions about television crews in my hospital, and I will only allow them with patient permission. You might be offering your services free—and we're grateful to have you here—but patient confidentiality will not be breached.'

Joe felt a shiver down his spine and a smile came to his lips. He might just love this older woman. There was a clear line in the sand. If Lien didn't like this guy, she would love this. He glanced over his shoulder. She was strangely absent, though he was sure she'd been around a few minutes before.

Joe kept out of sight, still listening to Hoa. The older woman commanded respect, and yet he'd seen her on her hands and knees cleaning vomit from the floor, and watched her playing games with some of the babies in the clinic.

Reuben had already shown little respect for the hospital and its staff. It seemed Hoa had already determined that he might act the same way towards their patients. She wouldn't tolerate that for a second.

Joe heard one of the nurses mutter something under her breath. He turned his head as he hadn't quite picked it up. 'What was that?'

The nurse rolled her eyes before turning her eyes back on the open office containing Reuben and Hoa. 'We've had his type before. Better start digging the grave in the back. Hoa will chew him up and spit him out.'

Joe let out a laugh. He couldn't help it. 'Well, show respect, get respect was what my old mentor taught me. For everyone—friends, colleagues and patients.'

The nurse smiled. 'Oh, don't worry, Joe, you're safe. We like you.' She gave him a strange knowing glance. 'In fact, we might have big plans for you.'

He put one hand on his hip as she started to walk away. 'Wait a minute, what does that mean?'

The nurse laughed and waved her hand as she kept walking. 'I'll let you know!'

Lien felt as if she were dancing some kind of complicated choreography. Every time she knew Reuben was in the clinic she made herself scarce. He hadn't deigned to give them his schedule to begin with, and just turned up whenever he saw fit. But Khiem took him aside and discussed with him the problems of co-ordinating patient care if they didn't know in advance that he was coming. Some of the patients that they wanted him to see lived far outside the city limits. It wasn't easy for them to reach the free clinic.

What complicated things more was the fact that the patients seemed to love the idea of being treated by the celebrity doctor, and all of them agreed to being filmed. This meant that the rest of the staff had to put up with film crews trailing through the hospital at inopportune times.

She could sense Joe standing at the door of one of the rooms in the ward today where she was sitting talking to a young mum. The woman was sick. Her blood tests and chest X-ray had revealed she was HIV-positive and had tuberculosis. Her lungs were under severe attack, and she'd only just been diagnosed; Lien was currently trying to balance a drug regime for both illnesses, alongside the pregnancy.

She held the young mum's hand and explained to her what her diagnosis meant.

This young woman had had no idea she'd even been sick. She'd been tired, and had a severe night-time cough.

She'd presented late into the pregnancy and been automatically brighter as soon as she knew she was pregnant—she seemed to think both of her other ailments were down to the pregnancy. Hoa had done the initial pregnancy booking, and a few simple tests had revealed the results that all the doctors had expected, with each disease speeding up the progress of the other.

Now the woman had developed a high temperature and breathing difficulties. She was thirty-six weeks pregnant, and both she and the baby were currently at risk.

Lien reached out and took the young woman's hand and spoke quietly and steadily, pausing to make sure she understood what Lien was saying and comforting her when it seemed appropriate. By the time she was finished she felt positively drained.

The young woman would be in hospital for the next few days. Hoa might even decide she needed a caesarean section if either the baby or the mum's condition deteriorated rapidly.

As Lien walked through to the office, she could feel tears brimming in her eyes. Some patients just got to her.

She walked in and closed the door behind her, expecting the office to be empty, then jumped when she realised Joe was sitting in a chair to her left.

'Sorry,' he said. 'I was just waiting until you'd finished.' He took one look at the expression on her face and jumped up. 'Lien. What's wrong?'

He didn't wait for her to reply, he just put his arms around her and pulled her into his chest.

She burrowed her head in his shoulder and just started to sob. Once she started she couldn't stop. 'I'm sorry,' she breathed. 'I don't know what's wrong.'

His grip was firm and comforting. She could feel the planes of his chest against hers. His voice was husky. 'You've got a really sick girl who should be celebrating her pregnancy. Instead, you've had to give her bad news. We both know she might not live to see this baby grow up, Lien. You wouldn't be human if you weren't upset.'

She sniffed and tried to wipe some of the tears away. 'But I know all this. I've dealt with it before. I should be stronger.'

He slid his hands to the tops of her shoulders and stepped back a little. He was still close enough that his breath warmed her forehead. She could see every little line around the corners of his eyes. 'You're strong. You're still here, Lien. You work in one of the most challenging places in the world and you love it.' He took a deep breath and gave her a sympathetic smile. 'There's always one that gets to you.'

She was still trembling. 'Who was yours?'

'What?'

'Who was the last patient that got to you?'

He closed his eyes. She actually felt him shiver as his expression grew dark. 'That's easy. A baby. A six-week-old baby with a spiral fracture in his forearm. Apparently he rolled off the bed and Dad reached out to grab him.'

Lien held her breath. She knew how rare spiral fractures were, and what caused them. 'A six-week-old baby doesn't roll,' she whispered.

He opened his eyes. 'No,' he breathed. 'I could have lost my job over that one. I put Dad up against the wall when he tried to grab the baby and leave.'

She shivered. 'What's wrong with some people?' She moved forward. This time it was her that wrapped her arms around him, hugging him tight.

His muscles were tense and it took a few moments for him to relax. After a second his hand went up to the back of her head, resting against her hair. It felt more personal.

She felt herself relax even more. She liked being in his arms. She could smell his woody aftershave at the nape of his neck. She could feel the muscles that lay underneath his lightweight top. It awakened senses in her that had been dormant for a while. One of her hands started running up the length of his back. As soon as she realised what she was doing, she froze.

He moved his head. And she lifted hers.

They were inches from each other. If either made the slightest movement their lips could connect.

It was unnervingly intimate. She was currently at work, standing in the arms of a colleague. She'd never done this in her life before. When she'd dated Reuben, they'd still been students at uni. Since then she'd only dated a few guys with other occupations. Never anybody related to her workplace environment. It was like her own little rule.

He blinked, and it broke the haze that felt as if it had descended between them. She couldn't help but feel bereft.

He gave a nervous smile and dropped his hands from her, stepping back. 'Sorry, you just looked like a colleague in need of a hug.'

'I was,' she said quickly. Then she took another breath and met his gaze again. 'And so did you.'

He broke their gaze and glanced towards the floor.

The silence seemed to last for ever. Did he want to say something else?

After a moment he lifted his head and cleared his throat. 'I came to speak to you about the prescribing regime for your patient. I'm unfamiliar with what can be prescribed for a pregnant woman with TB and HIV. I thought I should find out what protocols you have.'

Work. He'd turned this back to work. Her stomach flipped. She was uncomfortable. For a moment there she'd thought he might kiss her. She'd thought he might just lean forward an inch and let his lips connect with hers. She'd felt it. She'd almost tasted it.

What would she have done if he'd made that move? Would she have pulled back, or would she have responded?

Did she really want to admit the answer to that question?

She licked her lips and nodded. Work. This was work. 'Of course,' she said, her voice tight. 'Let's sit down. Hoa has made a flow chart for some of the protocols for pregnant women. There is a prescribing regime, but I actually planned to check with her once I got the results of some of the blood tests.'

Talking about work was easy. She knew she'd been tense this last week. Turning every corner in her workplace—her safe place—and wondering if she might see the man who'd told her she wasn't good enough was unnerving.

She'd no wish or desire to speak to Reuben again. But she'd heard he'd asked after her. How much could she realistically avoid him?

She stared at the paperwork in front of her, trying not to focus on Joe's strong hands as his fingers curved around the pen. What was wrong with her?

*Concentrate.*

Her brain was going places it shouldn't.

It had only been a hug, and she'd do well to remember that.

She held in a sigh and stared back at the protocol in front of her. For the first time in her life, she was tempted to mix work with pleasure. No matter how hard she tried, it seemed the logical part of her brain could only hear the pitter-patter of her heart.

This had disaster stamped all over it. Having Reuben around reminded her just how far apart her world was from Joe's.

What was that children's story—*The Prince and the Pauper*? That was how far apart they felt to her. No matter what his eyes had told her in that hug earlier. If he knew the truth about her, and her poor background, he would start to look at her differently, more coolly.

She remembered how that felt. How belittling. How sad it had made her.

And even though her brain told her all this, she could tell that her heart wasn't listening.

# CHAPTER SEVEN

THE TELEVISION CREW was like a virus. They seemed to spread everywhere, particularly into parts of the hospital they'd been explicitly told they weren't allowed.

On the other hand, the surgeries that Reuben had performed over the last few weeks were proving to be a miracle for some of the patients.

He didn't just do the showbiz plastic surgery. He'd performed a skin graft on a child who'd had her face scarred by boiling water. The early results were good. He'd also performed surgery on a woman with contracture of her fingers. For the first time in years she was virtually pain-free and had a hand she could actually use. He'd reset a woman's nose and fixed her shattered cheekbone after she'd been attacked by her ex-husband and had thought she'd be disfigured for life. Even from the sidelines, Lien's heart had tugged as the woman had seen her reflection once the bruising had subsided and had then flung her arms around Reuben in complete gratitude.

These were the moments for which Lien had become a doctor and, a long time ago, Reuben had made her believe this was also his reason for being a surgeon.

The cynical part of her knew that when the moment had been captured by the film crew, Reuben had achieved the best publicity he could possibly hope for. It wasn't a mistake. There was obviously another reason for all this, but so far Lien had managed to avoid him completely and now her curious brain wanted to know what he was really up to.

She and Khiem had been discussing two other potential patients for Reuben. One was a maternity patient who'd had an emergency section in an outlying village and had been left with a persistently leaking wound. They'd spent the last few weeks treating her underlying infection with IV antibiotics, and were hopeful that Reuben could use his skills on the scar and they could finally get the wound to heal.

The second was a child with a congenital condition who required facial surgery to assist his breathing. The surgeries were vastly different—but already the TV team were asking for permission regarding filming and publicity. It made Lien feel distinctly uncomfortable, but there was nothing she could do about it. Reuben was offering his time and services free, the hospital was picking up the aftercare. In any other set of circumstances these patients would never get the opportunity for surgery.

She'd just finished a ward round and was writing up a treatment regime for a TB patient when she sensed someone walk into the room behind her.

She hadn't even turned before every cell in her body froze. The confidence of the footsteps followed by the waft of familiar cologne was all it took.

'Why, there she is, the mystery doctor!' Reuben exclaimed.

She kept working. 'I'm busy,' was her brisk reply.

'Aren't we all?' He swept over to her with a swish of the white coat he persisted in wearing.

'What do you want, Reuben?' she sighed, still refusing to look up.

'Why, Lien? What's wrong? Anyone would think you weren't pleased to see me.'

'Anyone would be right.'

His hand closed over hers, and she was so shocked it took a second for her to snatch it away.

'Lien, why be like this? We were such good friends.' She couldn't quite work out if he was being deliberately sarcastic or if he really was so wrapped up in himself he couldn't see further than the end of his own nose.

'What are you doing here, Reuben?'

Now she did look up. He pretended to look hurt. 'Why do you think I'm here? I want to give a little back to the people of Hanoi.'

'And yet it's taken you six years to realise that is your calling.' The sarcastic words shot out before she had a chance to soften and rephrase them. She mentally cursed herself. It didn't matter how she felt about him, she still wanted him to do the surgeries on the two other patients.

It was so weird, staring into the face again of the man she'd thought she might have loved. It had been so long. His light brown skin had a strange sheen, his hair much darker than before. In fact, it looked a bit odd around his hairline. Years ago, Reuben's hair had been a bit thinner and he'd been paranoid about it. Had he had a hair transplant?

He'd always been good looking, but his face seemed different. Maybe he'd had some work done. She couldn't quite tell. The skin on his forehead and around his eyes was unusually smooth. Maybe some Botox? One thing was for certain, he'd had every single one of his teeth veneered. They'd been reasonably straight before, but now they were sparkling white and uniformly sized.

She laughed out loud. 'You look quite different.'

'I'm in the business,' he said quickly. 'When people come to see a plastic surgeon, they expect perfection. I try my best.'

'There was nothing wrong with the way you looked before,' she said quietly, and a little sadly.

His green eyes met hers. Even they looked different— a bit more startling. Was he wearing green contacts?

She sighed. How could she ever have thought they were on the same wavelength? She had no problem with anyone trying to improve their appearance if they chose to. But Reuben seemed to be trying to achieve an unrealistic perfection. That couldn't be healthy.

He waved his hand. 'Anyway...' his eyes swept up and down her body '...pleased to see you haven't let yourself go.'

She blinked, temporarily incensed at the entirely unprofessional comment. Her body was rigid and she struggled to keep her voice steady. 'Well, obviously my whole life depends on your approval of how I look, Reuben.'

One of his eyebrows cocked. She was surprised the Botox allowed it. They hadn't seen in each other in a long time and her obvious indifferent attitude to him wasn't sitting well.

She really didn't care. She was holding back—really she was. If she truly engaged her brain and her mouth he would doubtless walk out of here and never come back.

She took a breath. 'Tell the truth. What's going on— why are you really here?'

He leaned against the worktop, moving slightly closer

to her. He seemed to be under the illusion that she might welcome this.

'You know me, I'm just being civic-minded.'

She finished her chart. 'You're right. I do know you. At least, I do now. So, spill, Reuben. What gives?'

He looked down towards his handmade shoes for a second. 'I might need a little help.'

'Help with what?'

He straightened his back. 'It seems I might have some bad publicity heading my way. My publicist said that I should—'

'Your what?' She couldn't help but interrupt. She'd heard everything now.

'My publicist. She said that I should look a bit more civic-minded. It seems that some of the activity at the clinic has been examined. It was granted a licence on the grounds it would also see some local patients for free, but it's been so busy there just hasn't been time.'

She smiled. 'Ah, now we're getting to the real news.'

He lifted his hand to run his fingers through his hair, but they kind of got stuck.

'She asked me about my past, and if I knew anyone, and if there was some place I could think of to see some local patients.' He shrugged awkwardly. 'And your name came up.'

It was like a cold breeze sweeping over her skin. 'What do you mean, my name came up?'

He couldn't look her in the eye. 'Well, when she asked me if I knew anyone…'

'What, I was the one person who came from the worst district in Hanoi that you knew—the token person from the slum?' She couldn't stop the rage that surged through her veins.

The eyebrow remained raised. He seemed surprised by the passion behind her words. 'I know that you are familiar with the area, with the people—and their health needs.' He looked as if he was trying to find the right words, but there was an inherent smugness in how he sounded. He waved his hand dismissively. 'We know the stats. The people.' He glanced at her. 'The most deprived populations have the worst health.'

She put a hand to her chest. 'You mean *my* people?'

The words just came out. She hated the fact that her stomach almost curled in embarrassment or that she could feel tears prickling at the sides of her eyes.

'Well...yes,' he said simply.

She tried to push all her emotional and irrational thoughts to the back of her mind. She had to be professional. This was her workplace.

His hand swept past her again. 'I'm not all bad, Lien. You just think I am.' He put his hand to his chest and stepped a little closer, letting her inhale his cloying aftershave. 'I'm me. And you're you. We can't change that. But...' he took a deep breath '...I would rather fulfil the terms of my licence here than anywhere else.' His eyes rested on the stack of patient files on the desk. 'That tiny part of me that wanted to do well as a doctor? It is still there.' He shrugged. 'It just got lost in the hype. I know you have more patients for me. People I can help, who would never get these surgeries otherwise. People like you, Lien. I can be here once a week for the next four months. Will you let me help them, or should I go somewhere else?'

She hated him. She hated him for being so factual, and reasonable, but continuing to throw in subtle digs about their different backgrounds.

\* \* \*

It was quite extraordinary. When she'd started dating Reuben at university, he'd been a little pompous perhaps, but he had at least tried to fit in with all the other students. It had only been as they'd got further along in their studies that his entitled persona had appeared.

For a time Lien hadn't told anyone where she was from. Maybe she had felt a bit ashamed at the time— fitting in had been hard enough. It had been clear that most of the students who had been studying medicine came from well-to-do families. No one had known about her scholarship, and for that she'd been glad.

She'd been so focused on her studies that when Reuben had started to show an interest in her, and invite her on dates, she'd been quietly flattered.

After a few months of his endless attention she'd started to believe it was real. He'd invited her to his home and she'd been dazzled. When he'd asked about her family she'd made excuses.

It shamed her now to think about it, but she'd felt pressurised to fit in. She'd got along with the rest of her colleagues. Duc, Khiem and Hoa's son, had also been in her class. He'd been great, and he'd seemed to understand that she was trying to keep things quiet about her background. He'd never judged, or commented. Just kept gracefully silent. For that, she'd been eternally grateful.

Two years along it had been inevitable things would come to a head.

She'd noticed that Rueben had started to attend more and more events within his mother's elite circle—where Lien had felt distinctly uncomfortable. One night they'd been socialising with colleagues and he'd made some comments about those born in the 'wrong places', and she'd asked him to define exactly where he meant.

He named a few districts with a gesture of his hand— one of those districts had been hers. She hadn't waited. She'd exploded then and there, asking him what exactly was wrong with people from that district and not waiting for his answer before she'd told him that was where she had been born, and where her parents still lived.

The table had been shocked into stunned silence.

She'd realised what she'd done by the looks on some faces, but she hadn't been sorry. When she'd grabbed her bag to leave, Duc had joined her, along with a few other colleagues.

Two hours later she'd received a text from Reuben saying it might be better to break up. Even though she couldn't have agreed more, it hadn't stopped angry tears from spilling down her cheeks. The next day she'd discovered he'd transferred out of some of her classes.

She hadn't needed any more messages. He'd been embarrassed by her, and she'd been furious with him. She'd avoided him ever since.

He gave her an amiable smile. 'How about we look at these files together? You can fill me in on some of these patients.' He gestured towards the chairs.

Lien pressed her lips together. She should do this. She should do this for her patients. They had to come first, no matter how much she didn't want to be in his company. That was her problem—not theirs.

Once a week for the next four months wasn't actually enough. But it was more than he'd originally promised and it was a start. For now, she'd take it.

As she sat stiffly in the chair next to him, he gave her another half-smile. 'Oh, don't think I haven't noticed.

The other doctor, the Scot…is there something going on between you two?'

Her breath caught somewhere in her throat. She wasn't quite sure how to answer that question—she was caught totally off guard. But his words made old memories and feelings flood to the surface.

Feelings of how inadequate Reuben had made her feel. Would she feel that way around Joe too?

'Nothing's going on,' she said quickly. 'We're colleagues. I've been showing him around, helping him get settled in. That's all.'

Reuben gave her a knowing nod. It was clear from his expression he wasn't buying anything she was saying. 'Okay,' he replied simply as he pushed the first set of case notes towards her. 'Let's start here.'

# CHAPTER EIGHT

TWO WEEKS LATER, Joe and Lien headed to Uông Bí hospital to provide some holiday cover.

The car journey only took a few hours, with them mainly entertained by Regan singing at the top of his voice to the selection of songs he'd picked for the trip.

As they passed lush green hills with gorgeous scenery, Joe let out a sigh. 'This place is more like Scotland than I ever imagined possible.' He smiled and turned his head towards Lien, who was concentrating on the road ahead. 'I think it would surprise you. You should come and see it sometime.'

There was an odd silence for a few seconds. One that he wanted to fill. 'Ever thought about coming to Scotland to work for a while? You tried Dublin, didn't you? I bet we can be more hospitable. You should give us a try.'

Her jaw tightened, as did her hands on the steering wheel. 'I've done my travelling,' she said. 'I'm happy just to stay here now.'

Joe leaned towards her, his enthusiasm catching fire as he started to imagine showing Lien around the sights back home. 'You would love it. There are a few islands with cottage hospitals that you might like, or you could come and work in Glasgow with me. There are always positions for doctors.' He shot her another sideways glance. 'And we have plenty of space. You could stay with me and Regan.'

She shook her head as she drove. 'Nice offer, but I'm happy here. I don't want to work anywhere else. This is where my heart is.'

She said the words with an edge of determination. His stomach flipped. *Where her heart was.* Did that mean there wasn't room for anything else?

The thought was probably ridiculous, but as the seed grew in his mind he became even more enthusiastic about Lien coming to Scotland. He was sure she could love it just as much as he loved Vietnam. With Regan due to start school in a few months, he had to return. Was it possible he might be able to persuade Lien to join them?

'Glasgow and Hanoi aren't that different.' He gestured towards Regan in the back seat. 'Our life here isn't that different.'

Lien looked surprised. 'You're on a totally different continent, treating people with conditions you've never came across before, and speak a totally different language. How on earth can you find anything the same?'

He stared ahead and shrugged casually. He understood her points, but still felt the same. 'Patients are patients, no matter where in the world you treat them. They have the same expectations of you—that you treat them competently, and fairly, without judging them. For me, the hours are more or less the same, I have somewhere for Regan that I trust, and I'm getting to do the job that I love. The same as you.' He gave her a smile. 'We're not that different, you know.'

Her eyebrows shot upwards. 'We're a world apart,

Joe. You just don't see it yet,' she added with a hint of sadness in her voice.

He wasn't quite sure what she meant. In his mind, Lien was one of the most dedicated doctors he'd worked with. He'd hoped that she felt the same about him. Maybe he wasn't convincing her he was as dedicated to his work as he'd hoped. But he could work at that.

He shifted in the passenger seat. And he would.

She gave him a sideways glance and her lips hinted at a smile. 'Wait and see where we're going next, then tell me it's just like Scotland.'

He bit his bottom lip as he glanced at her again. Every day he spent around Lien he found himself more and more attracted to her—even though he hadn't acted on it. They worked so well together. He loved being around her. When ideas sprang into his head, she was the first person he wanted to talk to.

He smiled to himself. Lien had no aspirations to come to Scotland, but maybe he could persuade her. He kept smiling and settled back in the seat.

When they arrived in Uông Bí Lien took them for a quick drive around a few parts of the city, before driving out towards the hospital and giving Joe some background on the people who lived here.

By the time they finally pulled up in front of the hospital they were all ready to get out and stretch their legs.

The hospital was a more traditional building for Vietnam, made from wood, bamboo and cane, and set on stilts. Lien smiled as Regan and Joe looked up in wonder. 'Many homes in Vietnam are like this. Vietnam can be prone to flooding, so lots of houses built on flood-prone plains or in mountains are set on stilts.'

'Has this place been here a while?' Joe asked as he climbed the steps.

Lien smiled and nodded. 'We're like magpies. We tend to take over places that are a little run-down and neglected and take them over for ourselves.'

Joe's eyebrows shot up in surprise, but she laughed and shook her head. 'I'm kidding. The building in Hanoi was bought by Khiem and Hoa. This place was taken over and renovated by us after it fell into disrepair and the local community was requesting health care facilities. It does actually belong to us now.'

Joe grabbed the replenished medical supplies that she tossed to him and helped carry them up to the hospital. Her smile had got brighter with every mile of the journey and he could see the tension leaving her shoulders.

Lien opened the door to the hospital and showed Joe around. Even though it was set in a city, this hospital was very much on the outskirts and had a much more rural feel.

She showed them into a wide waiting room at the front of the building, with the back of the building divided into separate rooms. 'We have three consulting rooms, and six beds for patients if required. There is permanent staff here, so we generally only come down to cover holidays, or if there's some kind of outbreak.'

Two nurses came over to meet them and Joe quickly shook their hands and familiarised himself with the hospital setting and clinic arrangements. Lien appeared with a whole host of things she seemed to conjure up out of thin air. A pile of flat smooth rocks, along with some half-used bottles of paint for Regan. 'You paint these while your dad and I work, and once they are dry we can varnish them. You could send one of them back home to your grandma and papa as a present.'

'Wow, thanks, Lien,' murmured Regan. She'd also found some snacks and set Regan up in one part of the clinic where Joe could keep a close eye on him. Her thoughtfulness impressed him. She never forgot Regan, and it was clear that he appreciated the attention.

'We're ready.' She smiled as she moved over to the other treatment room with her nurse. 'Let's get started.'

Joe glanced outside. People were already forming a queue outside the main door. He smiled. It didn't matter where you were in the world—whether that was a GP practice in Glasgow or an outlying hospital in Vietnam—come opening time, there was always a queue of people waiting.

He nodded. 'Looking forward to it,' he said, and he meant it. The drive inside him that had disappeared these last few years had seemed to magically reignite the longer he stayed in Vietnam. It was good to feel this way again. He'd forgotten just how much it invigorated him.

He glanced around at the people. Lien was chatting away with one of the nurses, her dark hair swept up in a clip. Regan was engrossed in the corner of one room with his stones. Another nurse was setting out vaccinations on a metal trolley in the next-door room. He licked his lips, feeling the buzz deep down inside. Part of his interest was in the place and the people. His eyes went first to Regan; his son was happy here. He'd been happy in Scotland too, but somehow, now Joe could see new sparkle in his son's eyes. He was excited by the changes around him and seeing his son happy was feeding Joe's soul.

But there was something else. Something he couldn't ignore.

They'd been here three months, and the longer he was here, the more he was drawn to Lien. Everything about her pulled him in. Her work ethic, her passion, her drive, her sense of humour, and the electricity between them.

As he watched Lien, he couldn't stop the smile that had seemed permanently etched on his face since they'd all left Hanoi together. He hadn't felt this alive or happy in years.

A new determination spread through him. One thing was clear—now he'd found it again, he didn't want to lose it. When he and Regan boarded that plane back to Scotland, he wanted Lien to be sitting next to them.

Lien was happy to be busy. She always liked covering in the other areas because it gave her a wider feel for the health of the population. Sometimes it was nice to get away from the hustle and bustle of her own city.

Had Joe really invited her to Scotland, and to stay with him in his house/castle? She'd struggled to find words as the offer had seemed to come out of nowhere.

She couldn't deny the blossoming attraction, but he'd seemed to think the plan was easy. Did he really think she would just pack up and go with them back to Glasgow—to a country she literally knew nothing about? As for his house…

She shook her head at the thought. Her parents' house could probably fit forty times over into the place that Joe called home. She couldn't even imagine herself somewhere like that. The more she thought about it, the more she realised they were worlds apart. Just like she and Reuben had been.

She pushed all stray thoughts from her mind. The queue outside the hospital was getting longer. She was here to do a job and she had patients to see.

Halfway through the morning, things started to go downhill. The young man in front of her had muscle and joint pains, a headache and a fever. When Lien examined him he also had a widespread rash. He was clearly exhausted and going downhill fast. She asked if he had anyone with him and he nodded and pointed to the waiting room. 'My wife and son, they both feel the same,' he added.

Her stomach flipped. Her brain was already computing what was wrong and it wasn't good news, but from the look in the man's eyes he knew already what she would tell him.

She swallowed and put a hand on his arm. 'Give me a few minutes, Tadeus,' she said. She needed to chat with Joe. If she'd found one with this disease, it was likely there could be others. But Joe was just coming out of his own door to find her. 'I need to chat,' he said quickly. 'I think I've got two cases of dengue fever. It's most common in the rainy season here, isn't it?'

She nodded quickly, glanced in his room at the two patients, and at his notes. Dengue fever was spread by mosquitoes and was more common in the south of Vietnam, and in the wet season. Her eyes couldn't help but glance towards Regan. These people weren't infectious. The disease could only be spread by mosquito bite, but it still made her feel a little anxious.

'It does look like dengue fever. We don't wait, or rely on, the blood test for antibodies, we just go with the clinical symptoms.'

He nodded. 'But why here? Why now? Isn't it more common in the south?'

'Usually, but there can be lots of different factors. Just because it's more common in south—and in the rainy season—it doesn't mean that we don't see it at other times too. We'll need to ask about water storage, particularly if they store water in containers at their house—that can play a part in hosting mosquitoes.'

He scribbled some notes on the papers he had.

'How are your patients?' she asked.

'The mother has clinical signs and is tired, but I'm more concerned about the ten-year-old. He's clinically dehydrated and looks as if he could do with some IV fluids for a short spell.'

'Have they been anywhere unusual in the last ten days?'

Joe shook his head. 'Just at home.'

'Okay, I've got the dad. He's exhausted too, and a bit dehydrated. How about we hook up the father and child to IV fluids and some antipyretics for a few hours and assess them again. There's no widely available vaccine for this, no cure. We just have to treat the symptoms and hope they don't progress.'

He nodded seriously. 'Leave it with me. I'll take them all through to the ward and get things organised.'

Most international doctors would have left this to her, and it was nice to have someone want to truly share the load. It was like he could read her mind. He gave her a smile. 'My nurse, Eartha, will help me with the translations.'

He was trying to reassure her. 'I'll give you a shout if I have any questions.'

She was tempted to add more. To tell him about the

one or two per cent who developed complications. But somehow she had faith he'd already looked that up himself. She needed to let him run with this—he was more than competent.

Four hours later she'd seen a steady stream of patients. She kept being tempted to go and find Joe and catch up with him, but she knew that would look as if she was checking up on him. So instead she busied herself with putting a temporary cast on a broken wrist, prescribed antibiotics for everything from a severe chest infection, pneumonia and a kidney infection to an infected insect bite that really needed attention on a daily basis.

She also had a chance to catch up with a few long-term patients of the hospital who had tuberculosis, and a few with HIV. She always did her best to try and review the long-term patients to make sure they were keeping up with their treatment regimes and not suffering from any complications.

By the time she'd finished, Joe was waiting for her at the door, holding Regan's hand.

'How are things?' she asked.

'Both patients seem quite stable. They're going to stay in the hospital overnight and Terry will keep an eye on them.'

Lien nodded. Terry was one of the other local doctors and she trusted him completely.

'Let's wash up and we can go and find some dinner, then,' she sighed. 'Let's grab the car. There's a place just down the road that I like.'

They drove a little closer to the city and settled into a local restaurant half an hour later, but not before she'd made both Joe and Regan reapply their mosquito repellent. It hadn't taken them long to adjust to wearing long sleeves and trousers on a daily basis. Today's cases of dengue fever hadn't been unusual, but it still made her nervous.

Joe was surprised by her choice of restaurant. It was styled like an old American diner and even had a play area in the corner for kids. He glanced around at the street. It was dotted with a variety of international restaurants—some of them chains—but this one seemed a little more unusual. It was already crowded, with a host of locals and tourists.

'What?' she asked as she slid into one of the booths.

He shrugged as he slid in on the other side. 'I'm surprised this is one of your favourites.'

'Ah.' She nodded as she perused the menu. 'When I worked in Washington there was a diner that I loved. I swear they've stolen the chef's recipes and just transported him over here, because the burgers in here taste exactly like my favourite over there.'

He eyed the menu with caution. 'Okay, which one of these is your favourite?'

She pointed. 'The barbeque grand. Double stack with cheese, pickle, onion rings and fries.'

He laughed and she pointed to something else. 'If you're not that hungry you can always have the southern fried chicken burger. I like that too.' She paused a second. 'But if you're having that one, have it with the curly fries with cheese sauce and bacon.'

He shook his head. 'Where on earth do you put it all?'

'Hollow legs.' She smiled. 'It's a family secret.'

The waitress came over a few moments later and they ordered quickly. The lights in the diner were bright.

They'd booked into a nearby hotel for their stay. It was

comfortable and run by a local family. Joe was tired, but in no hurry to head back. Once they went back to their rooms he wouldn't see Lien again until the morning. This was the first time they'd had to sit down properly all day. Regan had made his way over to the kids' corner and was playing with a garage, dinosaurs and a pirate ship. Joe watched him for a few moments then turned to Lien. Since the moment he'd got here, he'd found her to be the person he wanted to talk to most—particularly when it came to Regan.

'I got a report from Regan's nursery teacher just before we headed down here.'

'Really? What did she say?'

He played with the cutlery in front of him. 'She said he's been doing great and has settled in well.'

She tilted her head to the side. That was the thing about Lien. She seemed to be able to read him so well. 'So why the long face?'

He leaned his head on one arm. 'They said that sometimes he takes himself off into the quiet room and just lies down.'

'The quiet room?'

'It's a space they keep in the nursery to allow kids to have some time out. It's got a library, and some cushions. The lights can also be dimmed and it has planets and stars painted on the walls.'

'What's bad about that?' Her question was reasonable. She made it sound so simple. But it didn't relieve the knot that had been churning in his stomach since the nursery teacher had talked to him.

He swallowed, his fingers drumming on the table. 'Regan told the teacher that he goes in there to speak to one of the stars because it's his mum.'

* * *

Her stomach flipped over.

'Oh.' She hadn't expected that. In all the time she'd been around Regan he hadn't mentioned his mum, and she hadn't wanted to bring it up.

His gaze met hers. 'Yes. Oh.'

She wasn't quite sure what to say. 'Is there a reason that he thinks his mum's a star?'

Joe nodded. 'I told him a story a few years ago, about how someone had bought us a star to name after Mummy, and that she would always be up there to talk to.'

Lien shifted a little in her seat. 'That's nice. And it seems a good explanation for a kid as young as Regan. So, what's wrong? Is this unusual for him?'

Joe's eyes looked sad. He interlinked his fingers and Lien got the distinct impression he was wringing them together. She could sense his low mood and frustration. 'He's never done this before. At least, he's never told *me* he does this. But he told his nursery teacher. What does that mean?'

Lien glanced at the happy little boy playing in the corner of the restaurant. He was currently involved in a great battle between dinosaurs and pirates, complete with sound effects. She reached her hand out to Joe's. 'It means he's a four-year-old boy who still wants to talk to his mum.' The truth was, she knew nothing about any of this. But she could try to think about this rationally.

'Now Regan's at nursery he probably sees other kids being dropped off by their mums and their dads. Maybe it's left him feeling a bit lonely. Maybe taking that time to go into the quiet room and talk to his mum, the way he sees the other kids doing, makes him feel less different.'

She put her hand between his and intertwined her

fingers with his. 'I know this is hard, Joe. I'm not an expert in kids—I'm not a parent. I can only tell you what I think it might be. Most kids don't want to be different from each other, even though they are in a million ways. I bet if you think back to your childhood or teenage years you can remember doing something that stopped you feeling different from others.'

Her heart squeezed inside her chest. For her, it had been in her late teens. It had been realising just how poor her family were, and all the different ways she'd tried to hide it from her friends. She'd tried to fit in every way she could. She had been pretty. And smart. Well mannered. When people had found out where she'd really come from—one of the most deprived suburbs in Hanoi—she'd seen them wrinkle their noses. And that was before all the stuff with her ex-boyfriend. He'd told her so many times how perfect she was—until he'd found out where she came from.

It had taken qualifying as a doctor and adulthood before she'd realised she should be proud of her upbringing, her parents, and what she'd learned in life.

Assumptions around poverty were made all over the world. Dang Van Lien made it her job to challenge them at every turn. She wasn't stupid. She wasn't dirty.

Yes, she'd been hungry at times. Yes, the house she'd been brought up in would have seemed like a slum to others. Her clothes had mainly been second-hand, most of her school books had been borrowed, and she'd spent her whole childhood finding ways not to require money. But she'd been brought up in a simple, tidy house filled with love. Her parents were proud people. Even though she'd offered to help them move, they didn't want to.

They'd told her on lots of occasions they had what they needed.

That didn't stop her buying gifts that were gratefully received. She'd replaced most of the household appliances and pieces of furniture as they'd broken down or had got to the stage where they couldn't be repaired. Every birthday and Christmas she bought her parents brand-new sets of clothes and a pile of books. Two years ago, her father had even accepted his first mobile phone.

She wanted to do more. She understood where the line was, and that by trying to do more she would insult them. Lien would never do that.

She squeezed Joe's fingers. 'Regan is a smart kid. And kids are more resilient than we think they are. He knows he has you. He knows he has his grandparents who love him. He also knows that his family is a little different from some of the other kids around him.'

She saw him blink and recognised the unshed tears in his eyes. Every instinct told her that Joe didn't normally let anyone see him cry. She could bet he'd shed a million tears over the loss of his wife, but Joe was the kind of guy to do that in private. His face for the outside world would be stoic. He was revealing parts of himself that he wouldn't normally.

Maybe it was being in a different country with unfamiliar people that was amplifying things for him. Or maybe he felt the connection between them that she tried her best not to think about.

She spoke quietly. 'Joe, I know this is hard. And I know there will always be dates, or occasions, in the future that will hit hard too.' She was thinking of special birthdays or Christmases. 'But I just want to tell you I think you're doing a great job. And Regan? He's a great kid. Smart, cheeky, with a big heart. You can't ask for more.'

Joe sucked in a deep breath and the expression on his face softened. The deep lines on his forehead smoothed out. He untangled their fingers and turned her palm over, tracing little circles with one of his fingers.

It was soothing. It was comforting. But it also sent a whole host of little zings up her arm.

Those green eyes met hers under heavy lids. 'How did I get so lucky?' he asked.

'With Regan?'

He shook his head. 'No.' His gaze was steady. 'With a colleague like you.' He lowered his gaze now. 'I don't like to wobble. I hate to feel that I can't be everything that my kid needs. On the few occasions I wobbled back home, my mum and dad helped paper over the cracks. We didn't talk about it. I'd just get up the next day to find my mother had crept in overnight and left a big pot of soup on the stove, or had done the mountain of ironing that I'd left. Or I'd get home from work and find my dad had mown the lawn that had been in danger of turning into a jungle.'

She gave a little laugh. The heat was spreading up her arm.

'Well,' she said softly, 'I certainly don't have—what do you call it, green fingers?'

He nodded and she continued. 'Neither am I particularly great with ironing. But I can tell you where all the best restaurants and stores are. I can find a thousand ways to amuse a kid without spending any money, and I can loan you another thousand bedtime stories.'

Joe sighed, and his finger kept tracing circles in her palm. 'I feel so weird about all this.'

'Why?'

He looked up, straight into her eyes. 'Us.'

Her back automatically straightened. Her mouth almost asked the question, *Is there an us?* But Joe started talking again.

'I feel as if I was meant to meet you. Meant to come here.'

She laughed. 'Your mother bought you the tickets.' She was doing her best to make light of this conversation because she was nervous. Nervous about what he might be about to say, or ask.

'She might have. But this time, this place…' He looked around and held out his hand. 'A crazy diner in the middle of Vietnam…it just feels…' he took a breath before the next word as their gazes meshed '…right.'

It was as if something unfurled inside her, like a flower bud opening to blossom. She could feel the heat spread out through her abdomen. She hadn't expected this. She hadn't expected anything. But she couldn't deny the crazy connection she was feeling.

She took a deep breath. 'You mentioned Scotland—'

She didn't get a chance to continue because Joe's eyes lit up and he started talking straight away. 'Yes. Think about it. Why not give it a try? The scenery is just as good as Vietnam.' He smiled. 'Maybe not the temperature. But there's so much to do. So much to see. Even I can't believe the similarities I see between Glasgow and Hanoi.' He reached over and grabbed her hand. 'I'd love to show you around Glasgow, just like you've done for me and Regan here. Who knows, you might even want to stay.' His eyes sparkled as he said those words and her heart sank like a stone. 'You can stay with us—we have plenty of room.'

She swallowed, her mouth dry. A few seconds ago their connection had felt stronger than ever as he'd told her about his worries about Regan. He'd confided in her enough to tell her that. She could see he was brimming with enthusiasm now and she couldn't find the right words. Their cultural and social backgrounds didn't just feel different at this moment, they felt like a vast abyss. She would never realistically leave Hanoi again—not for anything other than a holiday. Her heart rested here. With the people who needed her most.

She licked her lips. 'Thanks for the offer,' she said as casually as she could. 'Lots to think about.' She stopped there. She didn't feel up to this conversation going any further.

The waitress appeared with a bright smile and put the plates on the table with a loud clunk. Both of them looked up sharply and Lien pulled her hand back. Regan had obviously spotted the food because he appeared at their side. 'Is that my burger?'

'Sure is, buddy.' Joe pulled him up into the booth with them and shot her a quick smile.

She nodded back. This conversation had to be over for now. But as she picked up her knife and fork the turbulent feelings inside her stayed, and somehow she knew as she tried to sleep tonight her brain would be awash with a million other thoughts.

It was the first time he'd been openly affectionate towards her. It was the first time he'd looked at her and said the word 'us'. In just a few months he'd be going back to Scotland—with an expectation that she might want to go too.

And even though there was only a few inches between them, she'd never felt further away.

# CHAPTER NINE

'I DON'T WANT you to get too excited, but today we get a day off.' Lien appeared at their hotel room door just before seven a.m. She was smiling, standing in the doorway wearing a loose bright orange top and a pair of white linen trousers. Her hair was in a ponytail tied up high on her head.

Joe opened the door rubbing his eyes, but at her words he automatically perked up. 'What? Really?'

Lien nodded. 'We're just down here to cover for holidays. Plus, we're only about fifty kilometres from one of the most beautiful places on the planet—it's even a world heritage site.'

He wrinkled his nose. He was still waking up and his brain was playing catch-up. 'Where's that?'

'Hạ Long Bay. I feel kind of obliged to take you there and show it to you. Nobody should come to Vietnam and not see it. Plus there are some gorgeous hotels to stay in overnight, and watching the sunset there at night is just magical.'

He gave her a curious stare. For some strange reason he felt a sweep of jealousy. 'How often have you done that?'

She tapped the side of her nose. 'More often than you

need to know about.' She was teasing, he knew that, but it was strange how his brain was working. That sharp twinge of jealousy remained, along with a lot of curiosity.

'Can we go, Daddy?' Regan had appeared beside him and was instantly excited. 'Is there swimming?'

Lien walked over and bent down beside him. 'Sure there's swimming. Want me to take you in?'

Regan was already excited, jumping around. 'Yeah! Find my swimming trunks, Daddy. Let's go!'

Joe couldn't help but smile as he watched her bending down with his son. It was still playing on his mind—persuading her to think about coming to Scotland with him and Regan. Maybe today would be the perfect opportunity. Lien had a large brown paper bag in her hand. 'What's that?' he asked.

'Aha.' She gave them both a wide smile and opened the bag, letting the aroma of fresh Vietnamese bread spread throughout the room. 'This is breakfast. We can't start a day without snacks, can we?'

They piled into the car after finishing their breakfast and headed down towards the coast. Even though he offered to drive, Lien waved him off. 'Let me, I'm familiar with this road. It gets a bit twisty later on.'

She was right, of course, and while the busy traffic of the city wasn't quite replicated on these roads, there were still numerous motorcycles that seemed to dodge in and out of the sometimes stationary cars.

As they moved towards the coast the traffic built up again. Lien turned to them both. 'Okay, I have to warn you. This is an absolute tourist hotspot. This place will be busy.' She shot over her shoulder, 'Regan, you always need to hold someone's hand.'

'We have a few of these in Scotland too. Not World Heritage sights,' he said quickly. 'I mean tourist hotspots. The castle in Edinburgh practically buzzes with people. As do the Christmas markets.' He gave her a smile, as he could see them in his head, bright lights, decorations and the smells of chestnuts and wine. 'I think you'd like them.'

Lien pursed her lips. It was almost as if she hadn't heard those words. She, instead, continued their previous conversation.

She nodded ahead. 'The good thing is, you're here with me. I've booked us into a hotel just a little way up the coast that sits practically on the beach.'

'Doesn't it get overrun with tourists too?'

She smiled and raised an eyebrow. 'They don't take international bookings. They're not on any website to speak of. They don't need to. You can only book by phone and you have to speak Vietnamese to book.'

Joe pulled a face. 'Then how did we manage to get in?'

She patted her hand on her chest. 'Because you guys are with me. Plus they know Khiem and Hoa. Our doctors regularly have a night or two down here.'

She wound her way through some back streets and pulled up outside a hotel that was set on stilts like the hospital. Except this building looked very modern—it was white with large glass windows. They parked at the back and checked in at Reception.

'Don't look out of your bedroom window, you two, just get changed into your trunks, keep a T-shirt on, and I'll meet you back down here in five.'

Joe resisted the temptation to pull back the large white curtain from the glass doors in the room, and changed quickly, taking a few minutes to cover both him and Regan in sunscreen with mosquito repellent. He didn't want to take any chances, so he also threw some light long-sleeved tops and trousers into their beach bag.

Lien was waiting for them near the top of a flight of stairs. 'Are you ready?'

She was smiling as she waved them up. 'Take a look at what I think is one of the wonders of the world.' She smiled.

Joe stepped out. In front of them were hundreds of little islets in a bay of bright green water. Some of them were topped with thick jungle growth and a whole host of them were dotted all along the expanse of the bay. Further down, there were numerous boats, motor cruisers, Vietnamese junks and smaller fishing boats. A few rowing boats were bobbing underneath them along a wooden pier. 'Wow,' he whispered.

Lien's arms brushed against his as she leaned on the wooden railing alongside him. 'Yep—wow.' She pointed to the islets in front of them. 'There are more than sixteen hundred islets. They're made of limestone and they're all different sizes. Some big enough to have their own lakes, and a large number of them are hollow inside with gorgeous caves.' She sighed as she looked out across the bay. 'This beauty is the result of five hundred million years of tropical downpours.'

They stood for a moment just admiring the expansive view.

Lien nudged him. 'There are lots of tours and special cruises that go around the caves—particularly at night. Some of the caves are lit up in spectacular colours, oranges, purples, pinks. There are also lots of tours where you can go diving in the middle of the bay.'

She looked up out of dark eyes.

'Anywhere you can do that in Scotland?' There was the glimmer of a faint smile on her lips, even though it looked a little sad.

Joe shuddered. 'Only thing like this in Scotland is what we call the "stacks". Stacks of rock in the sea up and down the coastline of Scotland. Most are around the Highlands, and you definitely wouldn't want to swim in the sea there.'

Lien shuddered. This time her face brightened a little more. 'Let's stick to Vietnam, then.'

They stood watching as one of the sleek white cruisers, packed with people, prepared to head into one of the sets of caves in the distance.

'What are we going to do, Lien?' asked Regan, practically bouncing on his toes.

She bent down to speak to him. 'We are going to go down and take one of the rowing boats. See those islets out there? We can row over to any of them and explore. You pick.'

'Really?' Regan's head whipped one way and then the next. 'I can choose?'

'You can choose.' She beamed at him.

Joe's heart swelled at how sweet she was with Regan. And it came naturally to her, it wasn't forced at all. He could see that, and it made it more special.

He looked down at the array of boats. 'Have you done this before?'

'Of course. Lots of times. It's the best way to explore the bay.'

She held out her hands, one to Joe and one to Regan, and led them down the narrow path from the hotel to the bay. They climbed into the boat they chose, Regan laughing nervously as it rocked, and donned the life jackets inside. Lien leaned back for a second, closed her eyes and just breathed.

Regan shot Joe a questioning look.

Joe couldn't help but keep his eyes on Lien. It was almost like he was witnessing her little ritual. A wide smile spread across her face before she opened her eyes again.

Now it was all business. The business of fun.

She clapped her hands together. 'Okay, so we're at the quieter end of the bay. Like I told you, hardly anyone knows about this hotel in the fishing village. There are around seven hundred and seventy-five formations in a space of just three hundred kilometres in the main hub of the bay.' She turned to Regan. 'It's almost like a baker stood above it and sprinkled it with chocolate chips.'

He let out a laugh. 'Want to sit next to me and help me row?' she asked.

'Can I?' Joe could see the excitement gleaming in his eyes.

'Sure,' he said as he took his position at the other oar. Together they pulled away from where the rowing boats were moored and made their way across the perfect green sea.

'It doesn't seem real,' Joe murmured as their boat cut across the water.

It only took a few minutes for Regan to frown and say, 'This is hard work.'

Joe laughed. 'You think?'

Regan pointed to the nearest stack of limestone covered with thick green foliage. 'I pick this one.'

Both Joe and Lien laughed. She shook her head. 'Lazybones. There's another one, just a bit further out.

It's got a cave we can take the boat inside. It's like a private lagoon. I think you'll like it more.' She leaned forward and whispered in his ear. 'Maybe we'll spot some pirates!'

Regan gasped, a gleam appearing in his eyes. 'Row faster!' he exclaimed.

Around them other boats appeared. A party of around twenty kayaks glided past them, gathering at the bottom of one of the more impressive tall islets. 'It's a rock-climbing tour,' said Lien as they kept rowing.

'People are going to climb that?' asked Regan, his eyes wide as he tilted his head back and stared at the towering stack.

'Every day people climb that.' She nodded. 'This place is really popular with rock-climbers.' She paused and shipped her oar. 'Want to watch for a bit?'

Regan nodded and they shipped the other oar and leaned back in the boat, watching the intricacies of people attempting to climb a stack in the middle of the bay.

It took the climbers a while, and Joe reapplied their sunscreen and mosquito protection as they watched. Lien let him finish, then smiled. 'How about we take a dip in the water while we wait?'

Joe leaned over. The emerald-green water was clear, but he had no idea how deep the bay was. Lien must have read his thoughts. She tapped the life jacket she was wearing. 'Let's just keep these on,' she said. 'There are no currents around here, so we have nothing to worry about.' She turned to Regan. 'Will I go first, then you can jump in and join me?'

Regan nodded enthusiastically, so Lien positioned herself at the side of the boat, let out a yell, pulled up her legs and jumped.

It was a perfect dive bomb. Not at all what he was expecting. In his head he'd pictured her diving into the bay in one smooth move, but of course she was wearing a life jacket, and diving properly into the bay wouldn't work.

He already knew that Lien didn't need the life jacket—neither did he—but she'd wanted to make sure that Regan would be happy to keep his on, which was why she'd mentioned it out loud.

'Can I do that, Daddy?' asked Regan straight away as Lien pushed her wet hair back from her face and bobbed, laughing, just in front of them.

She held out her hands towards him. 'Come on, kid,' she said, her eyes sparkling.

Regan didn't hesitate. He let out a yell and copied Lien's dive bomb, flying through the air and splashing into the green water.

Joe automatically held his breath, waiting for the second when Regan would bob back up.

He sighed as Regan burst back up, coughing and spluttering. There was always just that moment when his irrational brain kicked in—fearing that something had happened to his son.

He knew it was ridiculous. He'd had to check himself a few times to stop himself from wrapping Regan in cotton wool. It was so hard. He'd already lost his wife, he couldn't bear it if something happened to his son.

But he didn't have time to think about that because Lien and Regan were shouting for him to jump in too.

'Come on, Daddy!'

'Let's go, slowcoach!' shouted Lien. 'What's up? Scared?'

She was laughing. He knew she was joking but, in a split second, his brain was interpreting the question in an entirely different way. Was he scared? Of course he was—but not of the water, not of the bay.

But of what was inside it.

Lien and Regan were splashing each other, carrying on, and having the time of their lives. He couldn't remember when he'd ever seen Regan interact with another woman like this.

He sent up a silent prayer. Thank goodness for this place. Thank goodness his mother had given him the push to step on the plane. Being in Scotland had left him feeling hemmed in. Here he was just Joe, the doctor. Joe, Regan's dad. Joe…the man who might actually consider looking at another woman, spending time with another woman.

His skin prickled. These thoughts had been dancing through his brain since he'd got here. But they'd only been dancing in the direction of one woman. A woman he'd already invited to visit Scotland with them. But Lien didn't seem quite so keen. Was he reading this all wrong? It had been so long for him that he wasn't quite sure how to do this any more. He took a breath and shook his head. It was time to stop.

He didn't let himself think any longer. He just jumped.

They splashed about in the water for a while, eventually tugging themselves back into the boat. Lien managed easily—she'd done it before. Regan scrambled up Joe's back as he held onto the side of the row boat. And Joe?

Joe's attempt to get back into the boat led to hysterical laughter from Regan and Lien with no help whatsoever. He kept getting one leg up, before the boat would tip towards him and deposit him straight back in the bay.

Eventually he ordered them both to the opposite side

of the boat as a counterbalance before he finally, inelegantly, flopped into the boat, not quite sure that his dignity was still intact.

'Looks much easier on TV,' he muttered.

Regan was still laughing so hard that Joe started laughing too. It was infectious. Seeing his son so happy and at ease.

When they finally recovered from their laughing fit, Joe helped Lien row over to an islet a bit further away. As they circled around the back they saw the large cave, which was hidden from view from the small beach. It was still daylight, but the streams of sunlight reflecting into the cave gave the place a magical green glow.

Regan's eyes were wide as Joe guided the boat inside. Lien had slipped her arm around Regan's shoulder in a reassuring way. She bent down and started speaking in a low voice. 'This is the pirates' lair,' she said.

Regan's head flicked from side to side as if he actually believed there could be pirates lurking within the cave. 'I don't see them,' he whispered back, his fists clenched in his lap.

Lien kept up the atmosphere as the boat bobbed further inside. 'They come here at night. Look at the groove in the wall. That's where they moor their pirate ship.'

'Their pirate ship fits in here?'

Lien nodded. 'It's magic. It gets to the entrance and squeezes down just enough so it can fit inside the cave and let them unload their treasure.'

'There's treasure in here?' Regan's voice rose in pitch.

'Oh, yes.' Lien nodded as she shot Joe a conspiratorial glance. 'Sometimes if you touch the inside of the cave, part of it will disappear and show you the pirate chest with all its gold and jewels.'

'Can we touch the cave?'

Lien smiled and nodded as she guided the boat over to one of the walls. 'Have a go,' she encouraged.

Regan stood up in the wobbly boat and pressed his hand against the wall, moving it in a few different directions. 'It's not working,' he moaned after a few minutes. He scrunched up his nose and pointed. 'Can we try the other side?'

Lien nodded again and this time Joe guided the boat to the other side of the cave so Regan could press his hands against the wall.

After a while Regan let out a sigh of exasperation and flopped back down in the boat. 'I can't find the treasure chest,' he said.

Lien nodded solemnly. She folded her arms. 'You know, there is a rule, but it's special. It's only for kids.'

Regan sat back up. Joe felt a little burn somewhere inside his chest. Regan was hanging on her every word.

He felt captured in this little world in the green-lit cave. In here he could forget about everything else. He could forget about everything that had gone before, the pain and the sorrow. In here, he could take pleasure in the connection that his son had made with Lien without wondering about what came next. Watching them together warmed his heart and his soul. If he could take this moment in time and put it in a bottle somewhere and keep it, he would. In a heartbeat.

'What is it?' Regan asked in wonder.

She put her hand on her chin. 'Well, it's said that if you can't find the magic treasure chest, and you're a kid, you get to make a wish.'

'What kind of wish?'

'A good wish. A lucky wish. Something to look forward to. Something that only you will know.'

Regan frowned. Joe could practically hear the whirring in his brain. He held up one hand, glancing between Joe and Lien. 'I've got it.' He looked really excited. 'How do I do it? How do I get my wish?'

Lien seemed to relish his excitement. 'It's easy,' she said. 'Lean forward and put both hands in the water. Once they're there, just say the wish inside your head. It's that simple.'

There was a swelling in Joe's heart. If only wishes were this simple. This easy. Regan stuck his hands into the water and closed his eyes. Joe could see him mouthing silent words over and over, but couldn't work out what they were. This place did seem almost magical. Joe wanted to believe that wishes came true in here too.

After a few tries, Regan sat back in the boat, looking pleased with himself. He nodded at Joe and Lien, then folded his arms across his chest. 'It's done.'

Lien was smiling, her gaze connected with Joe's. 'Then our work in here is done.' She pulled up the bag she'd brought with them. 'So, who's for some lunch before we go back out into the sun?'

The response was unanimous. They ate a leisurely lunch before spending a few more hours rowing across the bay and watching the various sights.

As they headed back to the wooden pier, Joe's hand closed over hers. He couldn't not say something. 'Thank you for today,' he said quietly. 'You made it really magical.' He paused for a second, then added the words that seemed to just spill out. 'For both of us.'

Her dark eyes were watching him carefully. 'Of course,' she said softly. 'Anytime.'

The buzz spread through him. It felt like pieces of a jigsaw puzzle were slotting into place in his brain—and he was finally getting to see the way the world should be, and all he could concentrate on was what he wanted to do next.

She'd had the best day. And she couldn't even begin to sort out why. If someone had told her last year that one of the best days of her life would be spent with a Scottish doctor and his son, she probably would have wrinkled her nose and said, *'What?'*

But there was something else. It was the way their gazes occasionally meshed, and in those few moments of silence it felt like a million unspoken messages were passing between them. She'd quickly learned to trust him at work. He did a good job, and queried anything he wasn't sure of.

After their tour of the bay, they went back to their rooms and rested for an hour, before dressing for dinner and dining in the hotel restaurant. Regan had been a relentless ball of energy all day, so it was inevitable that he would almost fall asleep in his dinner. So once they were finished, Joe carried him up to their room, got him settled, and then they met downstairs in the bar for a glass of wine.

The wide doors of the bar were open above the bay, letting the warm winds sweep in, and it was too tempting not to move outside and sit on the little beach just outside the glass doors of the hotel.

From this position they were almost directly beneath Joe's room. The windows and doors were firmly shut to keep out any mosquitoes but if Regan woke and flicked the light on, they would see it instantly.

All day today had been a bit strange.

Lien could almost feel the invisible cord pulling them both together. It was like a constant tug. If she ignored the little voices telling her that, socially, they were a million miles apart, she could easily let that tug take over.

Joe had started to look at her oddly at times. Almost as if he wanted to ask a question but was stopping himself from doing so.

She felt the same. How did you ask someone these days if they wanted to date? Was it even called that any more? Was she crazy to think about something like that?

They settled on the sand, her wine glass beside her and his beer bottle in one hand. For a while they just sat in comfortable silence. The bay was still dotted with little boats, and the green water gleamed in a variety of colours from the lights within some of the caves where people were still diving. It looked like something that should be on a postcard. After a few minutes of companionable silence Joe cleared his throat. 'Can I ask you something?'

Her stomach flip-flopped, wondering what came next. 'Of course you can,' she said as casually as she could.

'What do you want out of life?' The question was like a bit of a bolt from the blue. It wasn't exactly where she'd thought their conversation would go.

She pulled her knees up to her chest and stared out at the lapping water. 'I want to be happy. I want to be a good doctor.'

'Is that all?'

The words kind of stung. 'What do you mean, is that all?' Her brow furrowed. 'Is there a wrong answer to that kind of question?'

He closed his eyes for a second, and when he opened them again he looked at her in a way that sent tingles down her spine. 'What I meant was, is that enough?' There was almost an ache in his eyes.

'Why wouldn't it be?' Her voice was a little shaky now. She was treading so carefully. Fearful of taking a misstep. She hadn't been on the same journey that Joe had been on.

His fingers trailed along in the sand. 'I just wondered…'

'Wondered what?'

He didn't answer. He left those words hanging in the air between them.

The setting was beautiful. The sun was dipping in the sky, sending streaks of silver and lavender across the glittering ocean.

She couldn't help the pang in her heart right now. She'd never been this attracted to a colleague before. Something between them felt like it had just clicked. Her heart was currently ignoring the fact he was a mass of complications. He was a widower, who said he was trying to move on, but she wasn't entirely convinced. From what she could gather, his wealth was at the other end of the spectrum from her own family's. He was only here for a short time, and he'd already mentioned his intention to go back to Scotland. He was a single parent to a little boy. They seemed a perfectly contained little unit. There was no future here for either of them.

She and Joe seemed like they were a million miles apart in lots of ways. But she couldn't ignore the little stars that in her head were currently sparkling all around them—even if it was just her crazy imagination. Because that was how it felt, deep inside, like something bright and sparkly.

She actually wanted to laugh out loud. Her brain was obviously having a throwback to teenage hormones. This wasn't normal for her. Not at all. She'd guarded her heart very fiercely since the last time. She had no intention of letting herself be hurt again.

But as her brain filled with crazy thoughts, something else happened.

'I just wondered—' his voice was husky '—if it was enough. If you wanted more.' He put his hand up to his chest. 'From me, I meant. I wondered if your heart skipped beats the same way mine does whenever we're together, and if sometimes you think about me, the way I think about you?'

She couldn't breathe. She couldn't even gulp.

His green gaze met hers. Both of them were bathed in the dimming light. This could be a scene from a movie, and before she could think any further, Joe reached over and swept a bit of hair back from her face. The lightest touch of his fingertips made her lick her lips.

That was it. That was all it took. It was like a current flowing between them both and binding them together. She could see the same hunger in his eyes that was currently sweeping her body. In an instant, his head bent and his lips met hers. Her hand reached up automatically, her fingers threading through his thick hair. It made it real. This wasn't her imagination. This was really happening.

He wasn't gentle. There was a craving to his kiss. It felt like a test. One that she was determined to ace.

Her other hand reached up around his neck and he pulled her towards him. All of a sudden they weren't side by side on the beach any more. Her leg moved automatically so she was sitting astride him, letting her chest press against his.

His unshaven face scraped against her jaw, but it didn't make her pull back. Instead, it just seemed to light up her senses even more. His hands slid to her waist, one finger resting at the tiny break between her shirt and trousers, contacting her bare skin. It made her catch her breath.

She should stop now. She knew she should.

But she didn't want to.

She didn't want to be sensible. She didn't want to think about the trouble with mixing work and pleasure. All she wanted to think about was the here and now.

She'd thought about this. She'd imagined it. But her imagination hadn't even got close to how good the reality was. She could feel all her senses ignite. She pressed closer to him, wishing they were skin against skin. Her hands had gone from his hair and were now tracing down the broad muscles across his back. Her fingers itched to pull the shirt over his head.

As his hands slid up the bare skin at her back she let out a little gasp and tipped her head back. His lips went to her neck. To that tiny spot just below her ear where even the barest whisper of contact made her crazy. For a moment she was lost in the sensation. Lost in what might happen next.

'Whoa.' She put both hands on his chest and pushed back.

He stopped immediately. 'Lien?'

She let herself catch her breath. Her heart was thudding unevenly in her chest. His hands left her skin and went back to the sand. The first thing that struck her was how much she'd wanted them to stay where they were.

She gave a slow nod. 'I just need a moment,' she said huskily, gulping to try and let some more air in, to still her speeding heart.

'Sure.' He leaned back a little, giving her more space. She left her hands on his chest, letting the heat from his body permeate through her palms. She liked it. She could feel the energy, feel the buzz. This could be addictive. *He* could be addictive. Her own heart was racing in her chest and she could feel his doing exactly the same beneath her palms.

Her brain was trying to tell her to slow down and think. But she was tired of the voices in her head constantly reminding her how far apart she and Joe really were. She didn't care they were from different continents. She didn't care about their pasts. She didn't care how both families were at opposite ends of the financial spectrum. All she cared about was this buzz between them—this feeling.

She took a moment, breathing slowly, relishing what came next.

She let her fingers tap his chest before she lifted her head and gave him a smile. At any moment she knew she could stand up and walk away, but she didn't want to.

'Okay,' she murmured, tracing a line down his forehead and nose, pausing at his lips.

His face was serious. 'Okay...what?'

He was a workmate. She'd never mixed business with pleasure before. Every rational part of her brain told her to stop this now and walk away. But her thighs were practically clamped around his hips right now. It didn't matter what her brain said, her body had different ideas.

'It's fine,' he said softly, his accent broad. 'We can forget this ever happened. Write it off to two grown-ups getting carried away with the setting and the moment.' The hoarseness of that voice was setting pings off all over her body.

She shook her head firmly and twisted one finger through his hair. 'What if I don't want to forget it?' she said. She couldn't hide her teasing tone.

He straightened again, his hands leaving the sand and resting on her hips. 'You don't?'

Their gazes meshed. She could almost swear she could hear her heartbeat above the crashing waves behind them. 'What if my heartbeat races just as much as yours, and I think about you until I drive myself a crazy?'

A smile danced across his lips. 'You're sure?' he reiterated.

She said the words with complete conviction, 'I'm sure,' before leaning forward and pressing her lips to his.

# CHAPTER TEN

'DR LIEN, THERE'S an emergency!' The banging at her door woke her out of the perfect dream she'd been having of wearing red sparkly shoes and dancing down the yellow brick road. Joe had been there too, laughing and waving. Where on earth had that come from?

She rubbed her eyes as she strode over to the door and yanked it open. Her eyes caught the clock. Six a.m.

One of the nurses was at her door. 'What's wrong, Tan?' she asked.

'I'm sorry for waking you, but one of the kids that came in last night—he's taken a bad turn.'

Lien was already walking back to her bedroom to grab some clothes. 'Tell me more.'

'He's seven. Khiem admitted him with a type of malaria. His temperature had been really high and he had some infected bites. We started him on IV fluids and IV antibiotics. For a few hours we thought he was picking up.'

She'd finished pulling on her trousers and blouse. Her stomach had that sinking feeling as she quickly brushed her teeth. Over the last couple of years she'd managed to get dressed and out of the house within two minutes. As she crossed the grounds towards the hospital she twisted her hair up and fastened it with a clip.

A range of things was shooting through her mind. Japanese encephalitis? It could progress out of nowhere really quickly.

She'd only just made it onto the ward when Joe joined her. He was wearing jeans and a red shirt. Her stomach twisted. It was the one he liked to wear in bed.

'Where did you come from?' she asked.

He gave her a soft smile. 'Haven't you realised I've got a built-in radar when it comes to you?'

She returned his smile. Since coming back from the other hospital their relationship had blossomed quickly, and no one seemed surprised.

They never slept overnight in the same house but she often joined Joe and Regan for dinner, and frequently told Regan a bedtime story. It was always the small hours of the morning when she made her way back to her own house. They'd never really discussed it. There had been plenty of times when Joe had hugged her tighter and asked her to stay. But for Lien it didn't feel right. She didn't want Regan to wake up early one morning and find her in Joe's bed when he wasn't expecting it. She liked the way their relationship had been a slow burn.

It made it feel more real. More valuable. She'd got to know both Joe and Regan over months before anything had happened. They were friends first. He respected her. Getting to know him felt like peeling back layers. The big Scot was so much more vulnerable than anyone really knew—she suspected even his mum and dad. He hid it well. But the fact that he exposed little bits of it to her made her appreciate how close they were becoming. There were still parts of herself that she kept locked up—she continually tried to avoid thinking about the differences in their backgrounds. So she couldn't really expect him to tell her everything at once.

Esther's name was barely mentioned. Lien didn't like to ask questions. What she knew and what she'd learned had mainly been through casual conversations about something else, or from the little snippets that Regan occasionally blurted out.

His family were so welcoming. She'd already had an open invitation to visit Scotland from his mum and dad, and while that was lovely, it only made her feel more self-conscious. Could she really visit and be around people so obviously wealthy? She hadn't fitted in before, and she'd vowed never to feel like that again.

Joe touched her arm and smiled at her. There was an intensity to the gaze between them now, an intimacy, and every time he looked at her that way her mouth automatically responded. 'Tell me about our patient,' he said.

Tan appeared with the notes and gestured them both over to the room where the small child lay. She spoke quickly. 'This is Chinh. He was admitted last night with a fever and infected bites. He has malaria and has been on IV fluids and IV antibiotics with little effect so far. His heart rate has increased, and his blood pressure has dropped in the last twenty minutes.'

Lien went to step forward but Joe got there first. He touched the little boy's hand and his head shot round, his gaze fixing on hers. She could tell immediately he was concerned. 'What?' she mouthed.

Joe bent over the little boy and started saying a few words in Vietnamese to him, asking him how he felt, and if he could tell him his name, with little response.

He ran his hands over the little boy's arms, lifting the

sheet to look at his leg. Two of the bites on his lower leg looked particularly angry. One had a nasty thin red trail tracking just underneath the skin.

'Sepsis,' said Joe quietly, his head flicked to Tan. 'Do we have a sepsis trolley?'

Lien shook her head. 'No.'

He turned to face her. 'We have a history of skin infection, he's tachycardic, his breathing is shallow, he's confused and it looks like one of the bites is tracking. His hands are cold and clammy and his colour is poor.' He pulled his stethoscope from his pocket and listened to the little boy's chest. 'Shallow breathing,' he murmured.

He shot her a nod of acknowledgement. 'For me, this has to be sepsis.'

He gave her a few seconds. Her brain was racing. It had been a while since she'd seen a child with sepsis. Their deterioration could be very rapid as the infection raced through the blood, and the body's own overwhelming response could lead to tissue damage, organ failure and death.

She reached up and turned the IV bag around. 'These antibiotics clearly aren't working. Let's give him something else. Let's do something about that blood pressure too.'

'He needs an ICU,' said Joe in a hushed voice. 'Is there one nearby we can transfer him to?'

'Let me try and arrange it,' she said, tears pricking at the back of her eyes.

Sepsis could rarely be predicted but sometimes, if it was recognised early enough, action could be taken to stop it being fatal. Lien was praying that Tan had called them quickly enough to try and have some kind of effect.

She picked up the phone. Transferring a patient from

their hospital to the nearby ICU would be costly. May Mắn Hospital would be expected to pick up the cost as the referring hospital. The truth was, Lien didn't care about things like that. But life at the hospital meant making a decision that could affect everyone who worked here. It could mean fewer supplies, fewer facilities for the large population of people that they served. She could stop and wake up Khiem and Hoa to consult with them. But they trusted her. And she knew the decision had to be made.

She started speaking to the ICU, arranging the admission by speaking to the receiving physician, then booking an ambulance to transfer the little boy. Tan had already spoken to the parents—but they hadn't arrived yet.

Joe moved about, making up a new set of IV antibiotics and starting their administration. He monitored the little boy alongside Tan, charting everything carefully.

He was meticulous, and she was grateful for that, because she could feel herself starting to feel overwhelmed at the speed with which the little boy's condition was deteriorating.

The ambulance arrived and they helped with the transfer. The little boy's parents appeared just in time to climb in the back of the ambulance and kiss him before the transfer. By now Khiem and Hoa had appeared, with Hoa offering to drive the parents to the other hospital.

Lien waited until everything was done and the ambulance had disappeared in the distance before she felt her shoulders start to shake.

Joe exchanged a glance with Tan as he slung an arm around Lien's shoulders. 'Is there anything else that needs to be done right now?'

Tan shook her head and Joe nodded gratefully. 'I'm taking Lien for a break.'

He walked her back across the gardens to his house, settling her on the sofa while he woke Regan, got him dressed and fed him breakfast in extra quick time.

Regan was his usual chatty self and didn't seem to notice that anything was wrong.

Joe bent down and whispered in her ear. 'Do you want to wait here while I drop Regan at school?'

She shook her head. Her stomach was in such knots that she just wanted to get some air. 'I'll come with you. The walk will do me good.'

She still felt jittery. She couldn't stop thinking about the little boy. It didn't matter that Hoa had admitted him the night before. Lien had been on call last night. Maybe she should have gone over to the ward in the middle of the night just to double-check on the patients. Instead, she'd been in Joe's house—in Joe's bed—for a few hours before finally stealing back to her house in the early hours of the morning.

Tan had come for her this morning, but if Lien had been there, would she have picked up any deterioration earlier?

Joe held her hand the whole way to the nursery, and had his arm around her as they walked back, guiding her into one of the local coffee houses and sitting her at a table. She didn't even need to say what she wanted. An iced coffee and a bar of her favourite Vietnamese chocolate.

She'd expected him to sit opposite her, but he didn't. He sat next to her, putting his arm around her waist.

As she reached for her coffee she realised her hands were shaking.

'We need to give it a few hours,' Joe said. 'I'll phone to find out how he's doing. You know things will be hectic while they try to stabilise Chinh.'

It was almost as if he'd flicked a switch and turned on a tap in her. All her emotions bubbled to the surface. 'What if I missed it? What if I could have picked this up hours ago?'

Joe shook his head. 'It's sepsis. It's one of the most missed conditions in the world. It's only now that hospitals are really getting a handle on the signs and symptoms.'

She put her head in her hands. 'It was you who picked it up, not me.'

Joe shook his head. 'Only because I ended up a few steps in front of you. I've seen this. I've seen this before. Twice. As soon as I touched his cold hands my gut instinct just kicked in. You would have got this, Lien. I know you would have.'

She turned to face him, her emotions more raw than ever. 'But would I have? I should have gone back over last night. But instead I was distracted. I was with you.'

'What?'

Joe's face had fallen. He shook his head. 'We were together, Lien. You were still available at a moment's notice. You were still there if you were needed.'

She knew his words made perfect sense. But right now she just couldn't think straight. All she could think about was the little boy. She'd never seen a case of sepsis before. She knew it was worst in children and in the elderly, but she'd never seen a patient deteriorate so quickly.

She put her head back in her hands. 'It almost feels

like I could see his organs failing, one by one, right before my eyes.'

Joe's arm tightened at her waist. 'It's a horrible condition. It seems to come out of nowhere and it's vicious.'

He was still here. He was still supporting her, with his arms around her.

Even though she'd lashed out. Even though she'd almost blamed him for keeping her from her work.

Guilt flooded through her. If she'd been alone last night in her house, would she really have got up in the middle of the night, uncalled for, to check on the patients?

She reached out and put her hand over his on the table. She couldn't hide the fact her hands were still trembling.

Joe's voice was steady. 'Maybe you need a break. You work so hard. You're completely dedicated to the hospital. Maybe you need some time away.'

She felt instantly wounded by those words. 'Why would I want to be away from the place I love?'

Joe adjusted in his seat. He spoke softly. 'What I meant to say was maybe you'd like a holiday. A chance to be somewhere entirely different. Like…Scotland, with me.'

She froze. The tiny hairs on her skin prickled. Her brain felt as if it was spinning. This again. The conversation she kept trying to avoid. She shook her head. 'Scotland.'

It must have been the way the words came out but in her confusion she could see the wave of regret on his face. He looked down at the table. 'Maybe you need a change. I'd love you to join us. I can't stop thinking about this. I'd love you to come with us, Lien. Every time I bring it up you seem to avoid the conversation.' He pressed a hand to his chest. 'Tell me, Lien, am I reading this all wrong? I want to be with you. I can see a life for us together. You, me and Regan. Can't you see it too?'

She blinked. He was inviting her to visit in Scotland. The conversation that neither of them had actually had. But it felt all wrong.

'But you're going back. You're going back to put Regan in school. It's not a holiday, Joe. It's a relocation.'

He sighed and ran his hands through his hair. 'My time at the hospital will be up shortly. I'm sure that Khiem and Hoa have already recruited someone for this job. I need to go back home. Regan needs a chance to spend some time with his grandparents again.' He let out a long slow breath. 'I just wondered if you wanted to see a little of Scotland.'

Her insides were churning. Part of her had wanted this conversation to take place. She'd half dreaded that he might just step back on the plane back to Scotland and wave goodbye.

What she really wanted to do was throw her hands around his neck and try to keep him with her.

But life didn't work like that. He had a job back home. A house. A house that someone like her would never belong in. It didn't matter how welcoming his parents were. After a while they'd enquire about her, where she came from, and what her own parents were like.

Lien didn't want to leave them. She didn't want to live in a different country from them. How could she keep them safe if she wasn't here? How could she try to keep them healthy?

'You're going home, Joe. You're going back to your job, and your life. If I came—then what? You show me around Scotland for a few weeks then I come back here?'

'I guess that depends on you,' he replied. His gaze was steady, and she just wasn't sure if he was nervous about making any more suggestions.

She shook her head. 'I don't understand what you're saying.' Frustration swept over her.

Joe squeezed her hand. 'I guess I'm wondering what you'll think when you get there.' He gave a kind of hopeful smile. 'Maybe you'll love Scotland as much as I love Vietnam. Maybe you'll decide you want to stay with me and Regan. Work there.'

She could feel all her automatic defences slide into place. 'Because that's the only way we'll work—if I give up my life and come to Scotland with you and Regan? Scotland. A place I've never been, and know nothing about.'

He pulled back from her, grasping his hands together on the table and wringing them together. 'I don't know, Lien. I don't know how any of this will work. I'm trying to make sense of everything in my head. I'm trying to think of a way that this—us—doesn't actually end.'

Again her skin prickled and she took a deep breath. He was telling her that he didn't want this to end. Part of her heart wanted to sing. But it couldn't. Because in all his ramblings she hadn't heard any solution that would work for her.

Try as she may, she couldn't put the picture of his home out of her head. How many times over could her own parents' home fit into Joe's? Tears pricked at the corner of her eyes. She hated this. She hated those deep-down thoughts of not being good enough. It didn't matter how much she tried to shake them off, the adversity of poverty was ingrained within her. She'd learned to accept those feelings were there. She put her hands flat on the table, as if she was trying to steady herself. 'You know that I adore Regan,' she said steadily. 'And I would love it if you both stayed. But…' she shook her head slowly and willed herself not to cry '…I'm not sure that coming to Scotland is a good idea.'

'Why?'

'Because I can't stay, Joe. I won't stay. My life is here, in Hanoi. I've worked in a few other places for six months at a time. But I wasn't in either of those places to put down permanent ties. I always knew my permanent ties were here at the hospital. If I go to Scotland and stay with you and Regan, even for a few weeks…' she swallowed '…it gives him an unrealistic expectation of what happens next. He's a kid, Joe. He'll think we're playing happy families, and if I pack my case a few weeks later to leave again, what does that do to him? To his little brain? He's already got around losing someone he loved. How cruel would it be to walk away from him? I'm telling you upfront that I can't stay, but you're asking me to come without thinking about what message that sends to Regan.'

Joe bristled next to her. She'd never accused him of not paying attention to Regan's needs before, and this had obviously set him on edge. He went to open his mouth but Lien turned directly towards him and held her hand in front of his mouth. 'Would you want to tell your son that I don't love him enough to stay?' Tears spilled down her cheeks. She couldn't stop them.

Whatever words had been on Joe's lips seemed to die in the air between them.

His phone buzzed. A text from the hospital. But she wasn't interested in the text. She was interested in the fact that a few months on, his screen shot hadn't changed. It was still Esther.

It seemed so petty to complain about a photo of his dead wife. But it made her stomach ache in a horrible twisty way.

Joe seemed oblivious to it. He didn't even notice it any more.

But she did.

He reached up to brush away her tears but she shook her head and pulled back out of his reach. 'Don't.'

She couldn't bear him to touch her right now. Touching him would evoke all the memories that would make her crumble. His touch was proving addictive to her, and she couldn't go there right now. Not when she was trying so hard to be strong.

Joe's face looked broken. His voice came out of nowhere. 'Don't you love him enough to stay? Don't you love *me* enough to stay?'

Rage flooded over her like a tidal wave. 'How can you say that to me? How can you ask if I love you both enough to give up my whole life for you, when you wouldn't consider it for me?'

She pushed herself up from the chair. 'You're not playing fair. Why should I do this? Why should I be prepared to give up everything, go to Scotland and get my own heart broken when I have to leave?'

She leaned forward and willed herself not to breathe in. Not to inhale his familiar scent. 'What's so good about Scotland, Joe? What is it you need to go home to? Is it the memories—are you really ready to leave the past behind?'

She could sense he wanted to speak. But she didn't

want to give him the chance. She couldn't listen to him right now.

The thought of not seeing Joe and Regan every day was already niggling away at her. It wasn't a reality. Not yet.

But soon enough it would be, and she hated how much that pained her. She'd allowed herself to get too attached to them both.

She should have stayed away. Right at the beginning when she'd had that first little flutter of attraction, she should have pushed all thoughts from her mind. Instead, she'd let that attraction between them grow. She got more and more attached to that gorgeous little boy who looked at her with pure admiration and filled her days with joy. She'd allowed every flicker of a glance between her and Joe to build momentum. She'd reached the point where she ached for his touch. Even though he'd told her since he'd first arrived that he was only staying for six months, now it felt like a betrayal.

She knew it was irrational. She knew it was ridiculous. But her heart was overruling her head at every turn.

Part of her still wanted to jump at his invitation to go to Scotland. But every cell in her body knew it wasn't the right thing to do.

The ache at the bottom of her stomach sat like a stone. He still had a picture of his wife on his phone. He'd told her he'd come here to give himself and Regan a chance to move on. But his wife's picture was still there.

How would things be back in Scotland? She would be going into a home he'd shared with his wife. Scotland would be full of memories for him at every twist and turn. How on earth could she compete with those?

She shook her head. She didn't want to compete.

Here, Joe felt more like hers. Here, all the memories were theirs. No one else's.

It didn't matter that she'd always known he would leave. She'd stopped trying to think about it. Put it in a box somewhere in her head that she just didn't open.

But now it was here. It was the elephant in the room. Maybe this was why they'd both been avoiding this conversation.

She took a shuddery breath. Her hands wouldn't stop trembling. The tears were forming again.

'I can't do this,' she said rapidly as she pushed herself up and stepped away from the table.

'Lien, don't—' Joe was on his feet in an instant.

She shook her head. 'Don't. Leave me.' All the words just came tumbling out. 'I can't do this. I just can't. I don't fit in your world. You don't know me—not really. I can't go to Scotland and live in your castle with you. It's not me. It's not where I fit. And you don't have room for me in your life, Joe. You think you do—you tell yourself that—but the truth is you don't, you're not ready. I need some space.'

She wiped one final tear from her face. He looked aghast—as if he couldn't believe or understand what she'd just said to him—but she turned and fled the coffee shop before he could follow.

For a few seconds he felt as if he couldn't breathe. Had that really just happened?

He stared at his hands for a few moments, wondering how things could have gone so, so wrong. Every instinct in his body told him to get up and run after her. But she'd asked him not to. She'd asked him for space.

He had to respect that—even if he didn't want to.

He'd been nervous. His heart knew what he wanted. He wanted Lien. Every day he spent with her just reinforced that more and more.

He'd thought inviting her to Scotland was the perfect solution. The perfect solution for him and Regan.

He couldn't think about anyone but her. Her smile, her laugh, her fingers on his skin. The way she interacted with Regan.

Regan.

Part of the reason she'd said no.

He hated the way his guts were twisting right now. Being a single parent was hard. Asking someone else to come into your life meant they had to understand you were part of a partnership. Lien had sensed that right from the beginning. Most of the times they'd done something together she'd included Regan. She thought about him all the time, they had a connection together. One that had warmed his very soul.

But now?

She'd been clear. Part of the reason she wouldn't join them was because she loved Regan. She loved him. She'd said coming to Scotland and then leaving Regan would break her heart.

He took a deep breath. He'd been selfish. Somehow, because he'd told her from the first day they'd met that he was going back to Scotland in six months, he'd just assumed she wouldn't expect that to change.

He had already enrolled Regan in the local primary school back home. As the relationship between Lien and him had progressed he'd hoped she would consider joining them—that she would love them both enough to want to come.

But now he realised just how selfish that was. It was

clear she loved working here and was dedicated to the people that she served.

He'd made an assumption. He'd made the assumption that because she'd worked in some other places before, she would be prepared to do it again. For him. For Regan.

He shook his head and put his head in his hands. He hadn't even asked her—not properly—not until now, and then he'd handled it in such a clumsy manner. No wonder she was upset with him.

He hadn't even got the chance to take her hand in his and tell her how he loved her, and how much spending time with her had made his world seem whole again.

Something sparked in his brain. When she'd been upset, she'd told him he didn't really know her. What did that mean?

He couldn't even begin to imagine. He knew so much about her already. The way she drummed her fingers on her hip bone when she was impatient, the fact she lost a hair clip practically every day. She only liked one brand of jasmine tea, and she needed just the right amount of ice in her iced coffee.

The fact she loved it when he traced his fingers lightly over her back, or that her most sensitive part was just behind her ear.

How could she say that he didn't know her?

All he knew was that he loved every part of her.

He leaned his head back and closed his eyes. His fists clenched on the table in front of him. He had to find a way back from this.

He had to find a way to win the woman he loved.

# CHAPTER ELEVEN

THE LAST WEEK had been a miserable nightmare. Joe had tried to talk to Lien on more than one occasion, but had respected her wishes each time she'd just shaken her head and said no.

They had talked about hospital work and duties, but nothing more.

The dark circles under his eyes looked even worse than the dark circles under hers.

Regan had, at first, seemed oblivious and was still a little ball of energy around her. But even he'd noticed the change and wandered over one night and tugged her trouser leg. 'Why don't you come and tell me bedtime stories now?' he asked.

Lien crouched down to speak to him. 'I'm sorry, honey, I've just been really busy at work.'

Regan shook his head, his face solemn. 'No. That's not it.' He tipped his head to one side, his bottom lip trembling. 'Have I done something naughty?'

She shook her head and leaned forward to give him a hug. 'Of course not. You are the best boy that I know.' Her heart felt as if it were tearing in two. The last thing she wanted to do was upset the young boy who'd stolen a little part of her. She touched his cheek. 'Sometimes adults have to do other things.'

He wrinkled his brow. 'But if you can't do the bedtime story, you could still come and have dinner with us.'

She flinched. Everything was so easy when you were four years old.

Joe appeared at the door. 'Sorry,' he said quickly, holding his hand out towards Regan. 'I turned my back for a minute and he disappeared.'

'It's fine,' Lien said quickly, not quite meeting his sad eyes.

'But, Daddy—'

'Let's go, Regan,' Joe said firmly. 'Lien has work to do. You'll see her some other time.'

He led Regan back out and she watched as they walked back across the grounds to their house. She couldn't tear her eyes away. It wouldn't be long before they walked away for ever. How would it feel to be here and know that she wouldn't catch the familiar scent of his aftershave or hear the rough burr of his voice? She'd got so used to being around them, so comfortable.

But as they walked away, the void between them seemed wider than ever. Reuben appeared at her side, clutching some paperwork to add to the pile on the desk. 'Hey, Lien,' he said simply, shuffling the papers in his hands. He gave her a sideways glance. 'I meant to ask, how are your parents keeping? They live around here somewhere, don't they?'

Her skin prickled, her defences automatically on edge. It was a simple question. But one that she struggled to answer. Just that simple question flooded her brain with a whole host of thoughts about the differences in health between the richest and the poorest in Hanoi. It was likely he didn't mean it that way, but it sent a surge through her. She turned on him. 'Reuben, have you made a decision about what happens next?'

He seemed confused by the sudden question. 'What do you mean?'

She folded her arms across her chest. 'Long term. You said you'd work here for a few months. That time is nearly up.' She pointed to the piles of paperwork. 'There's still so many patients that could do with your services.'

He sighed and ran his hand through his hair. 'I know that. It's just the timing issue. I have other responsibilities, other priorities...'

She held up one hand. 'Shouldn't your main priority be about keeping your clinic licence?' She gave a casual shrug of her shoulders. 'If you're not working here—or somewhere similar—you're not really serving the needs of our population, and therefore not continually meeting your licence requirements.' She met his gaze steadily. 'Wouldn't you rather continue to have good publicity than bad?'

She hadn't said the words. She hadn't said she would report him or speak to the papers. But the unspoken implication hung in the air between them.

'You've got a good set-up here,' she continued. 'A good theatre and competent staff.'

Silence, then he took a deep breath, and let out a long sigh. His gaze met hers. 'It's nice to contribute to the health and well-being of the less fortunate,' he said smoothly. He paused. 'Maybe...two sessions a month on a permanent basis?'

'Two sessions a month would be excellent, Reuben.'

She dipped her head. 'The May Mắn clinic thanks you for your services to its patients.'

Her heart swelled in her chest as he walked out the door. Standing up to him had made her feel proud. A few years ago she could never have done this, but she'd already seen the differences his surgery had made to the lives of some of their long-term patients. This wasn't about her. And it wasn't about him. It was about the people who came here looking for help. The population she wanted to continue to serve.

She stared at the pile of paperwork on her desk. Referral letters, prescriptions to write and a few patients to review. Enough work to keep her here for the next few hours. At least then she wouldn't be sitting in her house, wondering what was happening in the house next door.

Her phone rang. She frowned at the number that flashed up on her screen. Her father. He rarely used the phone. It only took her a few minutes to realise something was wrong.

It wasn't her father that had phoned—it was her mother, and she was upset and babbling, talking so quickly that Lien could barely make out the words.

'What's wrong? Is it you, is it Dad?'

She tried to keep calm as she stood up and made a grab for her coat, the phone balanced at her ear.

'Yes, okay, does he have a temperature? Is he conscious? Can he hear you?' Her footsteps slowed a little. 'How long has he been sick? Why didn't you phone me sooner?' She grabbed her stethoscope.

Her heart was clamouring inside her chest. She kept walking. There was no point blaming her mother. She knew exactly what her dad was like. He didn't want to see any doctor—let alone his daughter.

He didn't ever want to admit that anything was wrong with him. It was just his nature and, no matter how hard she had tried over the years, there was no changing him.

'Mum, don't panic. I'm on my way. I'll be there as soon as I can.'

Tan frowned as she saw Lien rushing towards her. She raised her eyebrows in question, without getting a chance to say a word.

'I have to go. Emergency. I have to go and see...' She paused, not wanting to say the words out loud. 'A patient.'

'Which patient? Which area?' Tan started to walk alongside her. She grabbed hold of Lien's arm.

But Lien wasn't going to let anyone slow her down. She quickly gave her mum and dad's address as she bolted out of the door. 'Get someone to cover the hospital!' she added as she headed outside, looking up as lightning shot across the sky and the dark clouds opened above her.

Joe fought against the lashing rain that seemed determined to distort his vision. He was trying his best to use the app on his phone to direct him to the house that Lien had gone to.

He still couldn't get his head around this. She'd pointedly told him that they didn't make home visits, no matter what his objection. But she'd left the clinic without a word to him, and the only clue he had to her whereabouts was the note Tan had scribbled for him that had the address on it.

The streets here were narrow. Forgotten washing hung between the cramped rows, dripping enormous amounts of rain on him. Garbage cans were piled up all along the street, some overflowing.

Joe squinted again at a doorway just as someone pulled open the door and almost stumbled into him. The small man was clearly taken aback at someone nearly on his doorstep and started shouting at him angrily.

Joe took a few apologetic steps back with his hands raised. As the man continued Joe decided to take a chance and thrust the now damp piece of paper in his hand towards the man. He couldn't pretend he was anything other than hopelessly lost right now. The man looked at it for a few seconds and pointed to the other end of the street, continuing his rapid tirade.

After a few moments the man seemed to take pity on Joe's confused expression and switched to English. 'Last house, black door,' he said, before throwing something in a nearby garbage can, then pulling up his collar and hurrying down the street.

Joe sighed in relief and hurried down towards the black door. He lifted his hand to knock, and then paused. He wasn't even sure what to say. His Vietnamese was still sadly lacking, even though he'd tried his best to master the basics. He hadn't caught a word of what the other man had been saying to him.

A shadow moved further along the street. Another man, staring at him quizzically. Joe lifted his hand again and knocked sharply. Joe's stomach plummeted. He had no idea what this area was like. He'd sped out after Lien without a thought to his own safety. Lien's expression the last time he'd done this swam in front of his eyes—when she'd asked him if he would risk leaving Regan with no parent. He tightened his grip on the doctor's bag in his hand, wishing he'd taken the time to bring something less conspicuous. Trouble was, as soon as he'd heard that Lien had rushed out of the clinic alone, he hadn't hesitated to follow. There was no way he was going to leave her alone with an emergency. He knocked again. 'Hello, it's the doctor from the May Mǎn hospital. Is Dr Lien here?'

Lien froze. She'd just finished sounding her father's chest. His colour was terrible and his lips distinctly tinged with blue. It had to be pneumonia. She had to get him to hospital.

She was already cold from the pouring rain, but the familiar voice made every tiny hair on her body stand on end.

Her mother looked at her and frowned at the strange voice. Before Lien had a chance to stop her, her mother's petite figure had crossed the room and pulled the door open.

Joe stood in the doorway. There were only two rooms in the house so he could see Lien tending to her father as he still stood outside. He bowed to her mother and stepped inside. He had a large bag with him. 'What do you need?' he asked quickly.

She watched as he unloaded things he'd clearly brought from the hospital. A small oxygen tank, a pulse oximeter, along with an IV giving set, saline and a variety of antibiotics.

She blinked. She hadn't thought to pick up anything when she'd left. She'd been so panicked by the phone call all she had was the stethoscope around her neck and her phone in her hand.

Her hands started shaking as her father had another coughing fit. Joe took one glance. 'Is it pneumonia?'

She nodded. 'I think so.'

'Which antibiotics do you want to use?' he said.

She pointed to one with a trembling finger. Joe noticed, but didn't mention it. 'Why don't you let me set up the line while you tell the patient what's happening?'

He took a look around the simple home. She could almost hear his thoughts. Small, cramped. It was relatively tidy but the furnishings were worn.

He mixed the antibiotics, injected them into the saline bag, then ran the fluid through the giving set. She watched as he inserted a cannula into her father and quickly connected the bag, starting the process of delivering the IV antibiotics.

Her mother watched everything with wide eyes before finally starting to talk rapidly, gesturing towards Joe.

Joe's eyes were taking everything in. He still hadn't asked her any questions. He'd just come in and tried to assist. She watched as his gaze settled on a photograph in the corner. It was her. Dressed in her cap and gown when she'd graduated from university.

She saw him stiffen, the jigsaw pieces falling into place in his mind. He turned towards her, his mouth slightly open and his eyes wide. 'Are these your parents, Lien?' he whispered.

She automatically bristled becoming defensive. 'Yes, this is my mother and father.'

He reached into his bag and pulled out a tympanic thermometer. He held it up. 'Will you let your father know what I'm going to do?'

Tears pooled at the sides of her eyes. She had been so busy with the hospital the last few days she hadn't had time to see her parents. When her mother had phoned in a panic to say her father was unwell she'd just run from the hospital. She knelt beside her father's fragile body on the lumpy sofa and spoke quietly to him, before nodding to Joe to put the thermometer in his ear. It beeped a few seconds later and Joe turned to let her see the reading.

As suspected, her father's temperature was high. She'd already heard the crackling and wheezing in his lungs. The pulse oximeter showed his saturation level was low. Joe turned the oxygen tank on, and gently placed a filtered mask over her father's face.

'How soon can we get him to the hospital?' he asked.

She smiled tightly, mirroring the feeling in her chest. 'He won't go.' She let out a sharp laugh. 'He hates hospitals. He always refuses to come. I treat him at home for just about everything.'

She gestured to Joe's bag. 'I'd probably have had to go back to the hospital to collect some supplies.' She took a breath. 'Thank you for bringing them.'

Joe gave a nod. He pulled out some paperwork. 'Well, I guess you shouldn't really be prescribing anything for your father, so let me write the prescriptions.' He automatically started charting things on the paperwork. She watched the chamber on the IV drip, drip, drip the antibiotics into her father's vein, praying that this medicine would make a difference to him.

He was dangerously stubborn—always had been. He meant it when he said he didn't want to go into hospital. Any other person with an infection like this who refused to be admitted for treatment would probably die. She was pulling out all the stops for her father. Of course she was. But so was Joe.

The unlikely doctor from Scotland had made his way through the back streets of Hanoi to help her. To be by her side.

She wanted to believe that this meant something. She wanted to believe he wasn't just being a good colleague. The one part of her life she'd kept hidden. Now, for all her polite conversations, he could see exactly where she came from. But what if, deep down, he was just like Reuben and the thought of spending time with someone from such a poor background made him turn and run in the other direction?

Everything she knew about him said that wouldn't happen.

Every patient interaction, the way he responded to his son, his ideas for taking medicine to the people who needed it. It all told her he was an entirely different man from the one she'd spent time with before.

But those nagging self-doubts always persisted. It was like a tiny, insidious voice, whispering away inside her brain. No matter how much she tried to rationalise and push them away, they remained.

She hated them. She hated the fact they were there. She hated the fact that something that had happened years ago still had an impact on her life today. She was brighter than that. She knew so much better than that.

Reuben wasn't even a shadowy memory any more. He was a real, live, breathing person who she saw every week. She'd faced him down. She'd spoken to him. She'd even put him in his place. But still those horrible feelings of inadequacy persisted.

Would she ever get away from this? Would she ever be able to shake this off?

Joe continued to work away quietly, watching the monitors and her father's condition. He nodded gratefully when Lien's mother brought him some jasmine tea that she'd made.

He didn't even look at her, and the tiny hairs on her arms stood on end. Was he embarrassed by her background?

She looked at her watch. Time was ticking past and it was close to midnight. 'Maybe you should get back to the hospital,' she said quietly. Then her head flicked up. 'What about Regan? Who's looking after Regan?'

'Hoa,' he replied swiftly, 'and Khiem is taking care of the patients.'

He looked up and met her gaze. 'Everything is under control, Lien. This is where you need to be, and I'll stay as long as you want me to.' His voice was steady, soothing, like a warm blanket spreading over her shoulders.

He'd been asking to speak to her all week. Even now, he was letting her know that she was still in charge, and he'd only stay as long as she wanted.

He hadn't even tried to argue, or persuade her father about the admission to hospital that was clearly needed. She could tell from his face he didn't think this was the best idea, but it was clear he was going to respect her father's wishes and, in turn, hers.

With the storm raging outside, the temperature in the room had dipped. Lien's mother pulled out some blankets, tucking one around her father, then handed one to Lien and one to Joe.

She looked at Joe curiously and asked him his name. It was one of the few phrases that Joe had managed to conquer while in Vietnam. He gave Lien's mother a tired smile. 'Joe,' he replied as he shook her hand.

Lien's mother cast her eyes back to Lien as she shook her head, putting both her hands over his. 'Joe,' she repeated thoughtfully. 'Ah, Joe…and Regan?'

There was no point pretending that her mother didn't

recognise the name. Lien looked hurriedly at Joe. 'I've mentioned you,' she explained.

'You have?' He seemed shocked and she couldn't be surprised about it.

'I wish you'd brought us to meet them,' he added. 'We would have liked that.'

He said the words without a hint of criticism but with some disappointment. His gaze stayed on hers.

He didn't understand. He truly didn't understand her reservations and worries. He just looked hurt. As if she hadn't wanted to introduce him to her parents because there was something wrong with *him*, not with her.

Her father groaned and she moved quickly back to his side. 'Rest easy, Dad,' she said. 'It's going to be a long night.'

She pulled the blanket up around her shoulders and settled on the chair next to him, kicking off her shoes.

The rain thudded against the fragile window frame, already a few drops leaking in around the edges.

Joe stretched out his legs in front of him.

'Do you want to leave?' she asked, her stomach clenching.

He shook his head. 'Regan will be fine with Hoa.' He gestured towards her father. 'My patient is here. This is where I'm staying.' He raised a weary eyebrow at her. 'Unless I get thrown out.'

She wanted to smile. She wanted to smile because at one of the worst moments of her life he was here, and he was by her side.

But as she listened to the gurgling from her father's chest she knew the last thing she could do right now was smile.

It was going to be a long, long night.

# CHAPTER TWELVE

IT TOOK DAYS for Lien's father to get better. Pneumonia wasn't easy for anyone to shake off, let alone a patient with an existing chest condition with no real reserves.

Joe made arrangements with Lien so that both of them checked on him morning and night. At first she'd been surprised. But Joe could see the strain she'd put herself under. He wouldn't let any colleague do something like this alone. So between them they ensured the IV antibiotics were given, his observations checked, and they kept his oxygen supply topped up.

Joe had managed to exchange a few short conversations with Lien's mother. The woman was delightful, and seemed amused by his determination to conduct some of their conversations in Vietnamese.

By the end of the fifth day, Lien's father finally started to look a little better. His eyes fixed on Joe in a curious manner, and he managed to ask a few questions between coughs. All were signs of improvement.

He liked them. It was clear they didn't live in the best part of town. Their house was small, with most of their possessions showing signs of wear and tear. But they were a proud couple—particularly of their daughter. They spoke of her frequently when she wasn't there.

He could feel a real sense of determination about them. Somehow he already knew that any offer of help their daughter made would usually be refused. He learned that her father had worked in a factory for years but had been paid off when his health had failed. Her mother worked shifts in another place and frequently came home looking tired.

Joe knew better than to comment. His heart ached for Lien. If these were his parents, he would want to help too. But, he knew, in the same set of circumstances, his own parents would be equally proud.

It was a bitter-sweet cycle. They'd worked hard to support their daughter when they could, but wouldn't accept anything in return.

After five days he went to find Lien at the clinic. He needed that final chance to talk to her. He'd given her space like she'd asked, but he didn't want to leave Vietnam without telling her how much she meant to him and Regan, how much they both loved her.

One of the nurses gave him a wave. 'She's with a patient. She's putting in a chest drain. Why don't you take a seat in the office and I'll tell her you need to see her when she's finished.'

Joe nodded and sat in the office, his brain churning over what to say. He'd got it so wrong the last time. He couldn't afford to do that again.

He pulled his phone from his pocket and looked at the screensaver. Esther. He smiled. It had been there so long—for the last four years. He'd thought he would always want to look at it, to remind himself of the woman that he loved.

Yes, he would always love Esther. But he loved someone else now too. Moving on was done in lots of little

stages. He thought back to the day at the lake. They'd
asked someone to take a picture of the three of them
on the red bridge. The first picture had them all standing smiling. The second picture that had been snapped
had been much more impromptu, and had caught them
laughing when he had pretended something had jumped
from the water.

It was a moment in time. And it was his favourite
picture he had of them all.

It was time for a replacement. That was the picture
he wanted to look at every day. Life, love and laughter.


She felt jittery. She had to do this. She'd known this for
the last five days. He'd been good enough to help with
her father, and the least she could do was thank him for
his assistance. But it was so much more than that.

The thing she was dreading. This was goodbye and
her heart was already breaking.

She paused at the doorway, trying to steady her
breathing before she went in. Joe was looking at his
phone. Looking at the picture of his wife.

All the sadness and wistfulness rushed from her body.
If she'd had any hope that this was going to be anything
other than goodbye, it dashed out of the room like a bul-
let train.

Her insides coiled. This man she loved. This man
who had stolen her heart and asked her to go to Scotland with him was still looking at a picture of his dead
wife. Before, she'd tried to rationalise things. The time
for that was over. Now she was just *mad*.

'What do you want, Joe?' she asked coldly as she
strode into the room.

He turned, appearing surprised by her tone, and placed his phone on the desk.

'I wanted to talk to you. We leave in a few days and I can't go like this. I just can't.'

She folded her arms across her chest. 'Why?'

'Why?' He held out his hands and looked confused. 'Why? Because I love you, Lien, and I don't want to go home without telling you that.' He put his hand on his heart. 'Regan and I, we love you. You feel like part of us. Walking away from this feels awful. I can't imagine not seeing you every day. I can't imagine not working with you every day. I hate how things are between us right now. Tell me what I can do. Tell me what I can do to make things right. To make things better.' He stepped closer and reached out to touch her. 'Please, Lien. Tell me what to do. You're breaking my heart.'

It was all too much. All the things that had been nagging away inside her just bubbled to the surface, erupting before she could stop herself. All she could feel right now was rage. A few moments ago he'd been looking at his dead wife, and now he was telling her that he loved her. Lien just couldn't think straight.

'I won't do this,' she said, her voice shaking. She shook her head. 'I don't even really mean those words. But I won't be anyone's second best. I can't be with someone who still belongs with someone else.'

Now she'd started she couldn't stop. 'I don't want a bit of you, Joe. I want all of you. Yes, I'm selfish. No, I'm not prepared to share you with your dead wife and that sounds much more insensitive than I mean it to. You had a life. You had a child together. I respect that.

I respect the memories that you have, and want you to
share those with your son.

'But I can't be holding your hand, kissing your lips
or sharing your bed and thinking for a second that your
mind is with someone else.'

She pressed her hand over her heart. 'You told me
you were ready. Ready to move on. But are you? Are
you really ready? Because you're saying the words, but
it's as if your heart isn't quite there yet.' She shook her
head. 'I was a fool. I wanted this. Even though it took
me by surprise.'

He looked stunned by her words—as if she'd swept
his legs out from under him.

She took a deep breath. 'In a way—not just this—
other things have helped me make up my mind. Your
life back home. It's totally different from my life here.'

'What do you mean?' He still looked stunned.

She shifted uncomfortably. 'The house, the place your
parents live, the place where you live. It's obvious—'
she tried to choose the right words '—that you've all
done well.'

Joe frowned. 'What are you talking about?'

She sighed. She couldn't look at him right now. She
didn't want to see *that* look on his face. That one of quiet
revulsion. That one of not being good enough.

'You don't get it. You've lived a comfortable life. Not
everyone does that.'

He frowned. 'I know that. I work in one of the worst
areas of Glasgow city centre. Deprivation levels are high.
Poverty is everywhere. What is it you're trying to say to
me, Lien? That I don't know? That I don't understand?
Every time I see a sick kid in my practice I have to take
in all the things that affect them. A damp house. The

chaotic lifestyle of a parent.' He stopped and shook his head. It was as if something had clicked inside his head. 'No, no way. This is about your parents' house? Where you were brought up?'

She stepped forward and lowered her voice. 'It's not my past, Joe. It's my present. It's every part of me, and part of them. I've already experienced people rejecting me because they thought I wasn't good enough. And it's impossible to shake that off. My heritage is in my DNA. My childhood will shape the future of my adulthood. We know that now. We know that poverty and malnutrition in early childhood impacts on the health of adults. Even if I have money now, and do well, my body remembers. I don't know what's around the corner for me.' She shook her head. 'You don't get it. You just don't get it.'

The furrows in his brow were deep. His face was incredulous. 'You want us not to be together because of your upbringing? Where does this come from, Lien? Why on earth would you think that matters to me? Because I look as if I have a *posh* house back home? Because my mum and dad have one?'

He shook his head and stepped forward. 'I have a "posh" house because Esther and I had life insurance. When she died, I decided to put some money away for Regan's future and use the rest to buy the biggest house I could find. Something that didn't remind me of her at every turn. It doesn't *mean* anything, Lien.

'How on earth could you think I'd care about where you lived? Your mum and dad are two of the nicest people I've ever met. They are so, so proud of you, but they're also proud of themselves. I get it, Lien. I do. I know you want to help them more than they'll let you. But the most important thing was what struck me the moment I stepped through the door of their house. Maybe there wasn't money when you were a kid. Maybe you were hungry, and I'm sorry about that, but you had two parents who clearly adore you.

'We both know that for a child's health it's the most important thing. A loving, stable environment is the one thing that supports a child's brain development. Research shows it's the biggest thing that counts and you have that in spades. But if you didn't? That wouldn't matter to me either, because I love *you*, Lien, I know *you*. I don't care about everything else. I care about the fact that I want us to be together.'

She was holding her breath. He'd jumped all over the fears she'd held for most of her adult life. He didn't care. He didn't care about wealth and money.

Something passed across his eyes. 'Reuben.' He looked her in the eye. 'This is about that pompous ass, Reuben, isn't it? He treated you like that. He did that to you.' Joe started pacing. 'I never liked that guy. I heard the whispers, I knew he was your ex, and anyone can see that you don't want to be in the same room as him. That's why.' He shook his head again. 'Why didn't you just tell me the truth, Lien? Why did you think you had to hide your background from me? Why on earth would you think I would care about something like that?'

He lowered his voice almost to a whisper and looked up at her from under hooded lids. 'Is that really the kind of guy you think I am?' He looked wounded.

Her heart twisted inside her chest. She was confused. What he was saying to her confused her. As she stared into those green eyes she felt as if she could see right down into his soul. He'd told her the part of herself she'd thought she had to hide from so many people, and it didn't matter to him. And for that part she believed him.

But her heart still ached. While he might say he loved her, he'd still been looking at Esther's picture. She might know now that the house back in Scotland didn't hold memories of another woman, but she still felt she was in her shadow. She still felt as if Joe weren't truly hers. She might ache to have a life with him and Regan, but it still didn't feel right. Not really. Not when her heart was still here.

She shook her head. 'I love you, Joe, and I'll miss you. But I can't come with you to Scotland. There isn't a place for me there.' She put her hand to her chest. 'Not in here. Not where it matters most.'

Tears slid down her cheeks. 'Please don't make this any harder than I'm already finding it. I'd like to see Regan. I'd like a chance to spend some time with him over the next few days.' She gave a soft smile. 'I want him to take happy memories of Vietnam home with him.'

She tried very hard not to let her voice shake. 'And that's what I want for you too, Joe. I want you to take away happy memories of your work here, your time here. Because we've loved having you. You've played a huge part in the hospital over the last six months and we'll miss you when you're gone.'

She wiped a tear from her cheek and straightened her shoulders. 'Goodbye,' she whispered, then she turned away and walked on shaking legs out of the room.

# CHAPTER THIRTEEN

HE UNDERSTOOD EVERYTHING that she'd just said to him.

Alongside Regan, she was the first person he thought about every day. Somehow, when he blinked he saw her perfect skin, straight, shiny hair and cheeky smile, as if they were ingrained somewhere deep in his soul.

He hadn't come here looking for someone, but that was what he'd found. And he couldn't pretend it hadn't happened.

Home for him had always been Scotland. For the last four years he'd never looked any further. He'd never wanted to. But what if home could actually be somewhere else?

His life had turned upside down in so many ways. What if home wasn't the country he'd always lived in but instead where his heart lay?

Vietnam, and the woman in it, had captured him in so many ways. She'd woken him up in ways he hadn't expected.

When he'd got on the plane to come here, he'd fully expected to turn around in six months and head back to the home he owned, and the job he'd postponed back in Scotland. He hadn't really considered anything else.

And the truth was part of him was scared.

Could he live his life in another country?

Could he change his future plans for himself and his son?

He hadn't considered those things as part of his future. But now, discovering how much he loved one woman was making him reconsider his future in so many ways.

Part of the little seed of doubt inside him depended on a conversation he needed to have with his parents. He loved them both dearly. They expected Regan and him to fly back to Scotland and start anew.

Both of them were getting older. He wanted to be there for them, just like they had been there for him when he'd needed them most.

But his world had changed.

Places that had been smoky around the edges had sparked to life in a rainbow of colours he wanted to embrace.

And the person holding the key to those changes was Lien.

Of course she would have doubts. He hadn't even asked her the real question yet. Did she have room in her future for a Scotsman and his son?

All he knew for sure was that he loved her. Any plan that formulated in his head from here on included her.

Vietnam was a land of discovery for him. He wanted to stay here. He wanted to spend the rest of his life here.

And that realisation was everything.

It was the one option he hadn't given her. That they would stay here, with her. He smacked his hand to his head. Was he really that dumb?

He'd been asking her to upend her life for him when he hadn't offered to do the same for her. He knew that in her heart she felt she had so much work to do here. If he loved her, why on earth would he ask her to leave?

Lien was scared to trust him with her heart. He couldn't take back what he'd already lost to her.

He understood those fears. He understood that her whole future might look different from what she'd planned. Would she really be willing to share her future with him and Regan?

The fog that had enveloped him for so long had finally lifted. He wanted to reach out and grab the future, for himself, for Regan and for her. He just had to hope that her future looked a lot like his.

He pressed a button on the computer in front of him. He had to be honest and it started here.

Her legs were still shaking even though she'd lain down on her bed half an hour ago, curling up into a ball.

So much of her wanted to turn back and just say yes.

Joe and Regan made her happy. She was being selfish. One person couldn't have everything their way. She'd found love and family, maybe it was reasonable to have to sacrifice some of her career ambitions. But even just the thought of that made her stomach churn.

The knock at the door was something she truly wanted to ignore. She was always ready to work at the drop of a hat, but why today couldn't they find someone else?

The knocking continued, more insistently this time.

She rubbed her face, wondering if she should wash it before answering. But just as she swung her legs from the bed she heard the door open.

The footsteps were pensive.

'Lien?'

Her heart jumped.

Joe stood in the middle of the room with his hands at his sides.

'What are you doing?' she asked, staying at the doorway of her bedroom. 'I don't think my heart can take much more of this.'

'Neither can mine,' he said softly.

This time when he moved towards her she didn't object when he reached out to cradle her cheek in his hand.

'I'm sorry,' he whispered. 'I'm sorry that it's taken a broken heart for me to realise what was the first thing I should do.'

She frowned. 'What do you mean?'

She could tell he was nervous. His thumb brushed underneath her eye. 'I thought home was Scotland,' he said. 'I had never considered anything else. And I should have. Of course I should have. I don't want us to be apart. I want to spend my life creating happy memories with you, Lien. With you, me and Regan. If you'll have us.'

She shook her head. 'I don't get it.'

He smiled softly. 'Neither did I. But I do now. If we leave now, I leave my heart behind in Vietnam. I don't want to do that. This place?' He held up both hands. 'It's opened up a whole new world for me and Regan. We love it. The place, the people, the work, and—' he met her gaze '—one very special lady.'

His voice trembled. 'I don't want to go back to Scotland, because Scotland doesn't feel like home any more. Here, with you, feels like home.'

She held her breath. This was different. This was different from what he'd said before.

'If you'll have us—' his voice was still shaking and

there were tears in his eyes '—we'd like to stay. For good.'

She let out a gasp. 'What do you mean? I thought you had to take Regan home for school? What about your mum and dad?'

He nodded thoughtfully. 'Regan can stay in school here. He's learned so much already at the international school and he loves it. I'd be foolish to take him out now. As for my mum and dad...' He paused for a second, then reached up and cradled her cheek again. 'They told me to grab love with both hands and hold on tight. They love you already, Lien, and can't wait to meet you. They're probably booking flights as we speak.'

She blinked, tears flooding down her cheeks. 'But your job, your house...'

He shook his head. 'My house can be sold. I've rented it to the doctor and his wife who've been covering for me at the GP practice. It could be that they want my old job and my old house on a permanent basis.'

'You'd sell everything?'

He nodded. 'What do I have to go back for? We can visit my mum and dad whenever we choose.' He took her hand and put it on his chest. 'I want my life to be here, with you.'

'But...'

He pressed his lips together for a second. 'Maybe I'm reading all this wrong. Because if you don't want me to stay, I won't. I'm not trying to push things on you. But somehow I think that you love us, just as much as we love you.'

'You want to stay?' She almost couldn't believe her ears. Her heart felt as if it was swelling in her chest. 'You really want to stay?'

He nodded, and now a smile formed on his lips. 'Of course, Lien. We want to stay with you.'

Her hands started to shake. It was like the pieces of her life, and her heart, were finally falling into place.

'You're sure?'

He put both hands around her waist. 'You don't need to ask me that. I'm sure. Surer than I've been of anything. I won't change my mind. You don't need to worry about this. I love you, Lien. I asked Hoa and Khiem if I could stay. You know what they said? They asked when the wedding was.'

Her mouth opened. 'They, what?' She was shocked. It seemed like her colleagues knew her better than she did.

He moved a little closer. The solid warmth of his body was reaching out to hers. She wrapped her arms around his neck. 'So, what did you say?'

He smiled. 'I said it was all up to you. Pick a date.'

The love that she'd tried to fight for in the last few days finally bubbled over. She could love this man, and his son, all on her own terms.

She leaned her forehead against his, trying not to let her emotions overwhelm her.

'I'm sorry,' he whispered. 'I'm sorry you thought I was still living my old life. You caught me changing the picture on my phone that night—but didn't give me a chance to tell you that.' He pulled his phone from his back pocket and turned it around so she could see the screensaver. Her breath hitched. It was them, on the bridge at Hoàn Kiếm lake, laughing and joking together. 'This is how I hope we'll be for the next fifty years,' he said huskily.

She looked up into those green eyes. 'Just fifty?' she teased.

He closed his eyes for a second. 'However many we're blessed with.'

Now it was her turn to get it. And she did. He was accepting they'd take whatever time they had. Through his health or hers.

She ran her finger down his cheek, feeling his stubble under her fingertip. 'So…' she smiled '…about this date, how soon do you think your mum and dad will get here?'

'Dad!' Regan shot through the door, making them spring apart, laughing.

'Ooh!' he said, looking at them both, then putting his hands on his hips. 'Dad, were you kissing the girl?'

Joe laughed and swept Regan up into his arms. 'I was trying to. What's going on?'

Regan looked serious, as if he was trying to be grown up. 'I have a message. You missed Grandma and Papa video-calling. They said to let you know that they'd be here in three days and you need to find them somewhere to stay.'

Joe turned to Lien and raised his eyebrows. 'Three days?'

She wrapped her arms around them both. 'Sounds perfect to me.' And she kissed him, keeping her arms around the family that she loved.

\* \* \* \* \*

# LET'S TALK

# Romance

For exclusive extracts, competitions
and special offers, find us online:

f  facebook.com/millsandboon

⊙  @millsandboonuk

🐦  @millsandboon

Or get in touch on 0844 844 1351*

For all the latest titles coming soon,
visit millsandboon.co.uk/nextmonth